The
Golem
of
Old Prague

The
Golem
of
Old Prague

Michael Rosen
Illustrated by Val Biro

ANDRE DEUTSCH

For Harold and remembering Connie, Geraldine, Joe,
Naomi, Eddie, Laura and Isaac.

First published in 1990 by
André Deutsch Limited
105–106 Great Russell Street, London WC1B 3LJ

Text copyright © 1990 by Michael Rosen
Illustrations copyright © 1990 by Val Biro
All rights reserved

British Library Cataloguing in Publication Data
Rosen, Michael, *1946–* ✓
The golem of old Prague.
I. Title
823′.914

ISBN 0 233 98519 0 (hardback)
ISBN 0 233 98518 2 (paperback)

Printed in Great Britain by
WBC, Bristol and Maesteg

INTRODUCTION

Old cities are full of stories. You find them everywhere: two old men on a bench tell one before walking back home for their tea; girls skipping in a backyard sing out another for all the street to hear and then in the evening, after dark, two lovers slip across a bridge and giggle over an ancient story that, years ago, turned into a rude joke.

Sometimes curious people, with notebooks in their hand, sneak about, asking and listening – 'Do you know any stories? Can you tell me some?' When their notebooks are full, they leave them in cupboards or put them in special boxes and give them to old libraries.

The old city of Prague is a city full of old stories – some told, some sung and some hidden away in old libraries. For hundreds of years, many of the stories told in Prague have been about one strange, wise and magical man.

He was a leader of his people – but not one who wore a crown or led an army, because his people didn't have kings or armies. He was a Rabbi – a teacher, a scholar, a man who could help someone who was worried and advise people to do what was best. His name was Loeb (pronounced Lerb). Rabbi Loeb and his people were Jews.

Some of you reading this may not know who the Jews are. For several thousand years there have been people who call themselves Jews. Most of them have followed the rules and beliefs of a book called the Torah. There are five books in the Torah and they tell the stories of how the world began; Adam and Eve, Abraham and Isaac, Moses, Joseph, Sarah, Esther and many others that Christians and Muslims know as well.

During these several thousand years of following the Torah, the Jews have been part of many strange, wonderful and terrible things. The stories in this book come from four hundred years ago, when, like today, there were Jews living in most of the big towns and cities of Europe: London, Paris, Rome and many more. They had been there for hundreds of years working as trades-people like brewers (people who make beer), copper-smiths (people who make things out of copper), gold-beaters, carpenters and tailors; some worked on the land as peasants and farmers; some worked as merchants buying and selling things and some were bankers borrowing and lending money. Some were rich, some were poor; some went to pray and sing every week at the synagogue and celebrated all the holy days and festivals like Purim and Yom Kippur; others didn't bother so much, or believed in other things or became Christians.

At this time, the Jews in Prague lived in what was called a ghetto, a place where only Jews lived. It wasn't so much that no one else was allowed to live in the ghetto, but rather that the ghetto was the only place where Jews were allowed to live. Also, all Jews had to wear a special badge to show that they were Jews. It was a yellow star – the star of David, named after the boy who killed Goliath and later became the Jews' favourite king. In a place like this, the child who was to become Rabbi Loeb, was born.

Before the story begins, there's one more thing to say. The Jews in this book spoke to each other in a language called Yiddish, and at the synagogue in a language called Hebrew. You'll come across some Yiddish and Hebrew words in the story but right after them comes what they mean in English, like this: 'gut yomtov', have a good holiday.

CHAPTER ONE

The Birth

It was night time in the Jewish ghetto. All the shops were shut and the old narrow streets were empty. Tonight was Seder Night, the first night of Passover when every Jew would be at home having a wonderful time, eating, drinking, singing and hearing the Passover story.

Through the streets walked a man. You could hardly see that it was a man. He was wrapped up in an old cloak, his face hidden by a scarf. Across his shoulders was a big dark bundle. He seemed to be in a hurry but stepped carefully. Every so often he looked behind him and then, moments later, down the tiny side-alleys.

It was the Jewish year 5273, Christian year 1523, and Rabbi Bezalel and his family were sitting round the table. The room was bright with candles burning. Dishes of soup and dinner, and hundreds of sweet-meats were waiting to be eaten. Everything on the table was laid out there, as at all Passovers, for a special reason; to remind everyone in the room of the time when thousands of years before, the Jews had been kept as slaves in Ancient Egypt and then how they had escaped.

There were three pieces of matzo, a kind of bread that has nothing in it to make it rise like normal bread does.

There were roasted eggs and a bitter herb called Horse-radish.

'Oy, I remember it made my eyes water, last year,' thought the Rabbi's youngest son, Chayim.

There was a piece of roast lamb; some Charoseth, made of almonds, walnuts, cinnamon and apple; and there was some green parsley and lettuce. All of it there for a reason. All of it there every Seder Night.

Outside, in the dark, the man with the dark bundle hurried on.

The children, Chayim, Joseph and Esther were eyeing the matzos. Their minds were on the game they'd be playing later on.

First, mother breaks a piece up, then she hides it, and then we run about all over the place screaming, looking for it, remembered Joseph. I must win. I must win, he thought.

If we take a long time over it, Esther plotted, we go to bed really late – and no one tells you off on Seder Night.

There was a cup of wine, sitting all on its own. It waits for Elijah. He was one of the prophets, or wise men in the Torah and Mother had told them that he comes to every house to smooth out any troubles they've had during the year.

'What troubles have we had?' Joseph had said.

'Don't even ask,' Mother said.

And, there was a little bowl of salt water, to remember the tears that the Jews shed when they were kept as slaves in Ancient Egypt.

Rabbi Bezalel and the family began. The candles were bright and Chayim, Joseph and Esther teased themselves mad, thinking of all those sweet things they'd eat later. The Rabbi wanted his family to think of the times,

6

thousands of years before, when the Jews threw off being slaves and escaped as free people out of Egypt. He wanted everyone in the room to feel as if they were escaping themselves, that very night. He wanted them all to have a bit of hope in spite of the terrible times they were going through in Prague, with people making up lies about them and coming to terrorize them.

'This is the poor bread, that our fathers ate in Egypt,' he said. 'This year we are slaves, next year we shall be free men.'

The man outside, with the bundle, stopped, shifted his load across his shoulders and hurried on.

The youngest person in the room, Chayim, recited as loudly and clearly as he dared, 'Why is this night different from all other nights? Why is the only kind of bread we eat tonight, matzo? Why do we eat the bitter herbs?'

'We eat matzo,' the Rabbi told them, 'to remember the time the Jews were leaving Egypt; they were in such a hurry that they didn't have time to wait for ordinary bread to rise, so they took matzo dough with them. We eat the bitter herbs to remember those bitter times.'

And then he told them of how, when the Jews were slaves, they laboured away and built the houses but starved all the while. Then God brought down terrible punishments on the Ancient Egyptians: frightful plagues of frogs that died and rotted, boils that broke out on everybody's skin, locusts, flies and – the worst of all – the death of every first born child. Only the first born Jews were saved, he said, because the Angel of Death passed over them.

'That is why tonight is called Passover,' he said.

As each of these things were spoken of, they all leaned forward, dipped their fingers in a glass of wine and spilt a bit on the edge of their plates. The children giggled. They could smell their favourite noodle soup in the kitchen. It seemed such a long time to wait. So much talk.

The man in the street, reached a crossroads. For a moment, he couldn't choose which way to go – left or right? He chose right. He was heading for the Rabbi's house. He rushed on through the dark.

Rabbi Bezalel broke up a matzo and dipped a bit of the bitter herbs into the Charoseth and then put more of the bitter herbs between two pieces of matzo. And then everyone set to – 'At last!' thought the children – to eat the noodle soup, delicious potato pancakes: latkes, crun-

chy fried matzos, meat blintzes, cinnamon balls and that glorious stack of sweet things. Soon everyone was laughing and joking and drinking. What a great night this always was.

But then, at that special moment, just when they were about to open the door to let Elijah in, just as Rabbi Bezalel was reciting to God: 'Oh pour out your anger on to the people who destroyed the House of Jacob . . .' a moaning came from the Rabbi's wife.

'I can feel the baby coming,' she said, 'I can feel the baby . . .'

She was a full nine months pregnant, full term, as they

say. The Rabbi's house was full of poor people who had come to join the feasting when the Rabbi, as always had called out, 'He who is hungry come and eat!'

Two of them, an old woman called Rachel and her friend, Leah, rushed out of the house to look for a midwife.

'A baby on Seder Night!' Rachel said, 'Surely that's good luck, no? Though it's not such good luck for those who don't get to finish their meal and join in the singing and dancing.'

But also, at that very moment, there in the dark of the street, was the man, still huddled up, wrapped up in his old cloak, carrying the bundle on his shoulders. He was striding quickly towards the shouting, laughter and bright lights of Rabbi Bezalel's house. Just then, he caught sight of Old Rachel and her friend, Leah, spilling out on to the narrow street. He stopped, held still for a moment, slipped down a side street and then ran. But Rachel's friend saw him.

'Look there,' she shouted and they both saw the man slipping away into the shadows. They both knew, no Jew would be out on the streets on Seder Night and this was the ghetto where only Jews lived.

'You go for the midwife, I'll follow him,' said Leah and she rushed off up the street shouting, 'Stop, whoever you are, stop!'

The Night Watchman heard the shouting and, as luck would have it, he was coming towards them from the other end of the same street.

'Him,' shouted Leah. 'Him, stop him!'

The Night Watchman's eyes were tired and slow. His mind was full of how sorry he was that he wasn't indoors yet for the feasting.

'Stop him!' shouted Leah again.

10

The Night Watchman shook himself together and grabbed the strange figure as he tried to rush past.

'What's the hurry, stranger?' he said to the man, 'and what's in your pack?'

The stranger tried to wrestle free but the Watchman held on to him. Then as the man struggled, the dark cloth around the bundle worked loose. Looking up at it, lying across the man's shoulders, the Watchman had a terrible shock. He saw a small white thing. It was cold and still. Even in the dark, he could see what it was: a child's hand. The Watchman pulled back the cloth and he could see that the man was carrying just what he had feared he was: a dead child. Leah stared for a moment and then turned and hurtled back to the Rabbi's house. She knew what this was all about. The Night Watchman, meanwhile, marched the unknown man to a locked room for the rest of the night. From the houses all around came singing and laughing.

By the time morning came, Leah had been able to tell her story several times over; the Rabbi's wife had had her baby and the unknown man was brought before a judge.

'Such a night, such a night,' Leah kept saying over and over again. 'More things in one night than should happen in a lifetime.'

The judge began questioning the stranger.

'Where were you going last night?'

'To the cellar of Rabbi Bezalel,' said the man in a bold voice.

'Why?'

'To put the dead body of the child in there, of course,' said the man.

'Why?'

11

'So that these Jews might be known for the baby-killers they are,' he said.

'Were you alone in this?' said the judge.

'No, I was working with my friends, Spacek and Husak. We took the body of a Christian child from a new grave and I was going to leave it in the damned Rabbi's cellar.'

'Why?' said the judge.

The man started shouting. 'So that all the people of Prague and Bohemia might know that Jews murder our children at Passover time and use the blood to make their matzo stuff!'

'All that you have let the people of Prague and Bohemia know,' said the judge, 'is that you are a grave-robber and a liar. You and your friends will spend the rest of the year in the city prison and I, personally, wish that the Jews may spend the rest of Passover in peace.'

At the Rabbi's house, his wife had given birth to a boy. When it came for the time to name him, the Rabbi said, 'This child will comfort us. He came into the world to set us free from the terrible blood-lie that people say about us and our Passover matzos.'

He looked at the baby in his arms.

'We will call you Yehuda Liva after the great Rabbi of a hundred years ago who was in his time named after Yehuda Liva, Judah the Lion in the Torah, who, as it says there, will be praised by his people and feared by his enemies.'

And so, in the language of the people of Prague, the baby was known as Judah Loeb.

CHAPTER TWO

The Marriage

So Judah Loeb grew up and studied to be a Rabbi like
his father. He fell in love with a tall dark woman called
Pearl, a woman who people said was both lucky and
unlucky: unlucky because her father lost all his money
in one fell swoop in some foolish business affair – not
that that worried young Loeb who said he wanted to
marry Pearl, no matter how well or badly off her parents
were.

But why lucky? Pearl was not going to sit about waiting
for money to fall out the sky, she said. Instead, she set
herself up in a little shop, selling bread and salt and
whatnot. One day a troop of the royal soldiers came
marching through the streets of Prague: the horses strik-
ing the cobblestones, the harnesses jingling and swords
flashing. At their head rode a regimental major. The
column of troops passed Pearl's shop and, as they did so,
the Major thrust his sword into a great big soft loaf of
'cholla', the sweet Jewish Sabbath bread. Then, lifting it
up to where he sat on his horse, he pushed it into his pack.

Pearl screamed and called out to the Major, 'Don't take
my cholla without paying for it. I'm trying to make a
living here – and not just for me, you know, but for my

13

mother and father, too. They're too old to work them-selves. Please pay for that bread, sir.'

The Major looked through Pearl as if he hadn't seen or heard her. But then he pulled his saddle out from under him and threw it down in front of Pearl so that it landed on her counter with a leathery thud.

'I am hungry,' he said. 'I have no money to pay for your bread. Take the saddle instead.'

At that he rode off.

Pearl picked up the saddle, thinking, 'A saddle for a loaf of bread, not so bad, some would say. But what is a woman like me going to do with a saddle all of a sudden?'

Just then she opened up a wallet on the side of the saddle and there to her amazement were fifty gold ducats. She closed up the shop and rushed home to her parents.

'Mother, Father, look, look,' she said, and told them the story.

'And he didn't ask you to marry him, this Major fellow?' said her mother.

'What makes you so sure this Major was just a Major?' said the father to the mother. 'I tell you, it was Elijah himself, blessing the marriage of Pearl to Loeb.'

'I don't know so much,' said the mother, 'a beautiful girl like Pearl, he sees, and he doesn't want something for himself? He'll be back. Believe me, he'll be back.'

But he never did come back, and Loeb married the not-so-unlucky Pearl.

CHAPTER THREE

The Judgement

So Loeb became a Rabbi – but not just an ordinary Rabbi. He became one of the most famous Rabbis in all Europe. His name passed the lips of the most famous and brilliant people of his day. Among his friends were the great astronomers, Tycho Brahe and John Kepler. He became renowned for his clever thoughts and wise actions. He helped people who came before him and solved arguments between them.

In one large shop there were two little shops separated by a very thin wooden wall. One of them was owned by a neat little pork butcher, called Houdek who was, of course, not Jewish, because Jews don't eat pork. The other was owned by Polner, an old second-hand clothes dealer who, like plenty of other second-hand clothes dealers before and since *was* Jewish. The wooden wall between the two shops was splintered and cracked and the neat little butcher, Houdek, and the second-hand clothes man, Polner, could hear and even see what the other was up to.

One day Houdek the butcher put his eye next to a hole in the wood and watched Polner the second-hand clothes man counting out his money at the end of the day: the day's takings, as they say. The butcher made a note of exactly how much it came to, and then dashed off to the police.

'Fourteen gold ducats, four silver marks and forty-six groats have been stolen from me. I beg you to search the shopkeepers round and about where I work. I am sure one of them has robbed me of my takings, officer.'

The police hurried down to the market area and ordered every shopkeeper to stay just where he stood. Then, one by one they searched the shopkeepers' wallets and purses. When they came to Polner, there in his wallet were fourteen gold ducats, four silver marks and forty-six groats – exactly the same money that Houdek the butcher had said he had lost.

'Right, we'll have you,' said the police to Polner, 'you can come with us. You're under arrest.'

'But this is my money,' said Polner. 'This is the money I've taken from selling old clothes all day. This for the woman's hat, the silver for the breeches – it was a good price – they were leather.'

'That's easily enough said,' called out Houdek, 'I know, and you know you haven't had a customer all day, while I've sold ribs, chops, trotters and liver all day long.'

By now there was a crowd round, with everyone calling the odds, some saying Polner had stolen the money and some saying Houdek was lying. The two men were taken before a judge who, at the best of times found it difficult to remember which hand was right and which was left. He listened to the two shopkeepers and couldn't really make head nor tail of it.

His clerk whispered in his ear, 'Why not send for Rabbi Loeb, this is the sort of thing he might help out on.'

So, the Rabbi was sent for and came. The judge was happy to become a spectator.

'You sir,' Rabbi Loeb said to Houdek the butcher, 'do you have any coins of your own about you?'

'I do,' said the butcher.

'Fetch me two pans of hot water,' said Loeb to the clerk.

The court rustled with whispers while the clerk fetched the pans as soon as he could.

'Now drop these coins of yours into one of these pans here,' said Loeb, and Houdek did just that.

'Now drop the money that we are arguing about into the other pan,' he said to the police, and they did that too.

'And now we know the truth,' Loeb said.

There was silence. Heads turned towards each other with questioning eyes.

'Now we know the truth,' said Loeb. 'The second-hand clothes dealer did not steal the money.'

'Oh yes,' said Houdek angrily, 'and how do we know that? Magic? What are you? A witch?'

'No, my friend,' the Rabbi said, 'look at the surface of the water that has your coins in.'

Houdek stepped forward and looked.

'Well? What do you see?'

'Fatty stuff,' said Houdek.

'And how about the water in the pan where you put the money we're arguing about?'

Houdek looked again. 'Hmph,' he said.

'Well?' said Loeb.

'Nothing much,' said Houdek.

'Exactly,' Loeb said, 'then it can't be your money, can it? Your money has meat fat on it.'

Houdek stared around him at a court now full of smiles and nods. The judge and the police followed him to the pans of hot water to see the meaty grease on the surface of one and nothing on the other.

'So, my man,' said the judge, 'you have falsely accused this dealer in second-hand clothes. You have wasted my time, the police's time and this whole court's time – all for nothing. I won't send you to prison, that'll cost us even more. You can pay the very sum you say you were robbed of into this court and you can pay that very same sum to Polner the second-hand clothes dealer for the pain you have caused him. I don't remember exactly how much that was, but I'm sure you do. The court may rise.'

And everyone left the court laughing and mocking Houdek the butcher.

CHAPTER FOUR

The Disputation

Even though Rabbi Loeb was known and respected across the land, the old lies and rumours about the Jews still hung in the air like smoke on a still day. Many of them started out from the lips of a mad monk called Thaddeus. He was a good-looking, healthy-faced man who seemed to have grown strong feeding off stories about how the Jews killed Jesus; how the Jews killed Christian children; how the Jews were really the devil's servants. His whispers flowed amongst the people, turned into a flood that washed against the walls of the Jewish ghetto and threatened to engulf all who lived there. Thaddeus and his friends wanted the death of every Jew in all Bohemia.

Rabbi Loeb decided it was time to come out into the open about this affair. He sent a letter to the head of the Christian church in Prague, the Cardinal.

'I demand justice for my oppressed people,' he wrote. 'It is against God, it is against all humankind and against what Jesus said, to accuse the Jews of using Christian blood and to terrorize us on account of such lies. I request a public meeting where I might argue our case with you.'

The Cardinal replied, 'Your request is granted. Three hundred of our priests and scholars will put one question

21

each to you at a public place and this whole matter will be solved once and for all.'

Back went a letter from Loeb. 'My thanks to you for agreeing to hold this meeting, but three hundred priests and just one me is, perhaps, more than I can handle at one time.'

Loeb suggested a different arrangement, the Cardinal agreed and notices went up all over Prague.

GREAT DISPUTATION!!!
Rabbi Loeb, leader of the Jews will meet 300 Holy Fathers.
The Rabbi will debate with ten priests a day for thirty days!!!
Their deliberations will include:
God in Heaven,
The Death of Jesus Christ,
Christian blood and much, much more.

Starting tomorrow at 2 o'clock at the Dominican Priory and every day for thirty days
THE GREAT DISPUTATION!!!
CANNOT BE MISSED!!!

And so it was. Every day, Rabbi Loeb made his way out of the ghetto, through the streets to the Dominican Priory to face the questions. There in the Great Hall with its statues and old wooden carvings, hundreds of faces watched and listened to Loeb and the priests.

'Is it not written in your holy books,' said the priests, 'that you Jews need Christian blood for your Passover ceremonies? Is it not true that Jews killed Jesus? Does it not say in your holy books that Jews should hate Christians? How come the Jews call themselves the Chosen People?'

Loeb sat alone thirty paces or more across the stone floor from the team of priests asking the questions. The faces in the hall frowned and nodded. Clerks scratched away as fast as they could writing down all the Rabbi's answers, and these became so famous that they were kept and can still be found hundreds of years later, deep in the libraries of the Dominican monks of Prague. There they can be read, the answers he spoke out in the great hall, surrounded with that audience of priests, monks, nuns, bishops and people from the court: dukes, princes and ladies.

'We teach in our books that no blood of any kind at any time can be consumed by a Jew,' said Loeb, 'so why would we want blood in our food at our most sacred of times, Passover?

'But more than that,' he went on, 'we teach that he who raises his hand in anger against his neighbour – even if he doesn't actually hit him – is a wrong-doer. We are not in the business of killing people. But yet more than this too: we say there is nothing more important in this world than trying to keep someone alive – even the Ten Commandments may be put aside if it means that someone who is dying might live a moment longer.'

The priests sat behind a great oak table, listening closely. For each answer he made, Loeb told them in which holy book they could find these things. Pages turned even as the Rabbi spoke.

'Jesus died,' said Loeb, 'because his father let him die. His father is God himself, the Supreme Judge. How can you say the judges on earth, the Jewish judges killed Jesus when the Supreme Judge let him go to his death?

I ask you this, who was really in charge that day? The Jews or God?'

Whispers and mutters rose and fell like waves. Priests' heads drew close and then separated again.

'Didn't your church begin because Jesus died?' Loeb went on. 'Isn't that why you have a church? So how come you go about being angry with us for the death of Jesus? Shouldn't you be thanking us for sentencing him to death so that you could start your church and religion? Shouldn't you be thanking us for doing what God wanted?

'Even so,' he finished, 'does it say in your Bible that the Jews killed Jesus? No. Who does it say did it? The

Romans. You accuse us of doing something we didn't do.'

As the Great Disputation went on, day by day the name, Rabbi Loeb, could be heard across Prague, Bohemia and beyond in monasteries, churches, market-places and innyards. At the end of the thirty days, there were no more questions from the priests' table. All Loeb's three hundred questioners came together in the Great Hall along with courtiers in their finery, and any other person who had managed to beg or bribe a way in. Loeb came to a close, the last question answered. For the first time in thirty days no words passed across the stone space between the priests' table and Loeb's chair. With no sig-

nal to command it, the three hundred priests rose to their feet and clapped. The Cardinal stepped forward and shook Loeb's hand.

'Your answers have taught us many things. I shall tell all my priests throughout Bohemia what you have said. I hope that from this day, now and for evermore there will be peace between Jews and Christians.'

Out went the town criers:

'RABBI LOEB ANSWERS THE QUESTIONS!!! CARDINAL AND RABBI IN HISTORIC AGREEMENT!!! PEACE BETWEEN CHRISTIANS AND JEWS!!!'

'Peace? Never,' laughed Thaddeus when the town criers' words reached his ears. 'Is there peace between God and the devil? No. Then why should there be peace between Christians and Jews?'

CHAPTER FIVE

The Kaiser

Rabbi Loeb came back to the ghetto his mind still busy with all the words and thoughts of the previous month. He was greeted there as a hero by hundreds of fellow Jews. The streets were full of people laughing and patting each other. Little dances broke out on street corners. Loeb had put a stop to all the lying talk. Such a clever man, so wise with his words, people said. As if all this hadn't been extraordinary enough, the next day, through the gates of the ghetto, drove the Royal Messenger's coach. It rattled to a stop at the doors of Loeb's house. Two footmen crisply jumped out, and handed Rabbi Loeb a card. The Rabbi's presence was requested at the Emperor, Kaiser Rudolf II's palace. Loeb rushed to tell Pearl, there was a flap and a flurry around the house and Loeb bundled himself up in his robes, climbed into the Royal carriage and found himself skimming through the streets to the palace. All the people in the ghetto looked on, and wished him well.

Three hours later he was back, his house full of friends and well-wishers waiting with eager ears to hear what had happened.

'The Kaiser spoke to me for about half an hour,' said

Loeb, 'and gave me his royal word that from now on he would root out all rumours and whispers of the blood-lie in Bohemia. He says he will treat Jews just as he treats all other people in his kingdom and will protect our rights to be merchants and trades men in the city.'

The room shook with the cheering. Complete strangers kissed each other. It felt to them as if Loeb had led them out of a prison into a field of flowers. When the cheering and kissing died down a little, Pearl, Loeb's wife, spoke up.

'So half an hour you were with the Kaiser, Judah Loeb, what of the other two and a half hours?'

The Rabbi was quiet for a moment, then said, 'What took place in that other time shall never be spoken of by me or anyone else.'

A silence fell on the room. What could it have been, people thought, and why can't the Rabbi say?

And so it has stayed, a great secret down through the years until a few years ago, a Jewish scholar was rummaging through old manuscripts in the attics and cellars of the old ghetto when he came across a bundle of writings by none other than Pearl herself. Well, perhaps the great Rabbi Loeb did say that what took place between him and the Kaiser would never be spoken of, but, as often happens in cases like this, there was one person he had shared the secret with – his wife.

Pearl wrote: Kaiser Rudolf said to Rabbi Loeb, 'I feel a strange and troubling struggle inside me. It is as if two people are fighting in my head. One of these people hates Jews with a deep loathing but the other feels drawn to any Jew I happen to meet. It causes me disturbed nights, strange dreams and hours of unhappy moods. One moment I want to march my troops into the ghetto, order

28

them to draw their swords and kill every Jew in sight; the next I find myself madly in love with a Jewish woman I have glimpsed from my coach, or I am longing to be locked in discussion with a Jewish scholar, like you, Loeb.'

Loeb listened to this story and then asked for a few moments on his own. After a short while, he spoke to the Kaiser.

'I have seen your life,' he said, 'I have seen the life before your life.'

'And?' said the Kaiser.

'Your parents were not happy together. Your father could not join with your mother to make a child. Your father blamed your mother for this. There were quarrels and bitter times. Your mother grew to be afraid of your father and feared that he would throw her out of the palace. She wondered, how could she become the mother of a child?

'Her eye fell on a very fine-looking young man who was often to be seen at the court. He was a Jew who came to do business with the Chancellor. Your mother sent him a note asking him to come to her private room without being seen or telling a single soul. When the young man arrived, she looked down the passage-ways and into the alcoves to check that no one was spying on them. When she was sure that they were completely alone, she told him that she had fallen in love with him.

'I hoped that this feeling, in time would pass; but instead it has grown stronger and stronger. You live in my dreams,' she said, 'and yet when I wake up, it is as though you are still there beside me in my bed. I beg of you to make that dream real, and come to me where I sleep and be there when I am awake.'

'Your Highness, the young man couldn't believe he was hearing these things from your mother. She was a very fine looking woman and the young man was excited by what she was saying. He would have loved to have said yes to everything she asked him to do.'

But, as Loeb explained to the Kaiser, 'The young man was very religious, or as we say, "frum", your Highness, and no matter how much he would have liked to have done the opposite, he backed away from your mother. He said, "I cannot do what you ask, no matter how much I might feel that I would like to. All that I know and have studied teaches me that it would be wrong for me to do such a thing. I am a Jew, you are a Christian. You are married, I am not. We cannot make love in secret for even if no other human being knew of it, God Himself would know."

'Your Highness,' said Loeb, 'your mother flared up in anger and yelled at the young man, "If you don't listen to me and take notice of what I am saying to you then I will go to my husband and force him to send out instructions that every Jew in all Bohemia should be destroyed."

'The young Jew left in a terrible state not knowing what to do. Should he do something that was against the law of God? He took his problem to the Council of Rabbis for them to decide.

' "What should I do?" ' he asked them.

'They talked about the problem until late into the night. In the end, they decided that it would not be wrong for the man to do what your mother had asked. He would save the lives of many Jews, wouldn't he?

'The young man said, "Put that in writing and sign it."

'And when they had, he thrust the piece of paper into his robe and hurried back to the palace. He tried to keep

31

his face from showing the feelings he now had for your mother but you can be sure it showed. He met your mother secretly in her private room. We do not need to go into details but you, your Highness,' said Rabbi Loeb, 'are the result of that secret meeting.'

Kaiser Rudolf could hardly believe this story and said so.

'Do you know which room was your mother's private room?' said Loeb.

'Indeed I do,' said the Kaiser.

'Then take me there.'

Together the two men, the Kaiser and the Rabbi, made their way up to a tiny room in a far corner of the palace. It was locked, but the door was old and broken. With their shoulders, they forced it open and staggered into the room. It was dusty and empty. An old tapestry that had been on the wall lay on the floor where it had slipped from its rail years before. No one had been there for decades.

'Lift this board,' said the Rabbi.

The Kaiser bent down and levered up a loose floorboard in a corner of the room where a bed had probably been. There, resting in the dust was an old vase. The Kaiser lifted it and then hesitated. The Rabbi motioned him to carry on, so Rudolf put his hand into the vase and brought out an old browned piece of paper. On it were written the words of the Council of Rabbis, granting the young Jew permission to do whatever the Kaiser's wife asked him.

The Kaiser turned to Loeb and said, 'I feel as if a great load has been lifted from my shoulders. All those strange feelings fighting each other inside my mind have gone. I owe you a great debt.'

There Pearl's old manuscript ends. Now we know why Kaiser Rudolf II had been so kind to the Jews that day in Prague. On that day the Jews celebrated and danced and sang in the streets.

Away in a corner, Thaddeus plotted.

CHAPTER SIX

The Feast

As you might imagine, after this, the Kaiser grew to be quite fond of Rabbi Loeb and the two men began to see each other more often. Loeb was invited to the palace for long discussions with learned judges and the famous scientists of the day. One of the Kaiser's ministers, a pink sweaty man, was a close friend of Thaddeus and together they began to scheme how they could wrong-foot this Rabbi who seemed too clever by half.

'Your Highness,' said the minister, 'all your ministers and courtiers have arranged wonderful festivals and feasts for you. However, your new friend and companion the great Rabbi Loeb, doesn't seem to have been quite as generous as the rest of us. May I suggest that you test whether this man really is worthy to be your friend and trusted follower?'

'And how should I test him?' said the Kaiser.

'Why, by ordering him to lay on a grand feast for you, my Lord.'

The Kaiser was tired of his ministers sneering and sniping at Rabbi Loeb behind his back, so he thought maybe if he agreed to their suggestion, it would deal with all this nastiness once and for good.

'Very well,' the Kaiser said, 'I will see Loeb today.'

When he did and told the Rabbi of the proposal, Loeb said, 'I will do as you wish, your Highness, but please can I have four weeks to prepare the banquet?'

'Of course,' said the Kaiser.

He returned to the jealous minister and told him that the whole thing was under way.

The minister burst out laughing. 'How can he prepare a feast for a Kaiser? The man is poor. He has no money. He is desperately trying to keep pace with our style of life here at the court. Of course, he can't keep up and now mocks you with promises he can't possibly keep.'

'We shall see,' said the Kaiser.

'We shall see that the man is, like all his kind, a liar,' said the minister.

Over the next four weeks, the minister regularly sent a secret messenger to spy on Loeb to see what he was up to. Every day the messenger came back to the minister with the same story:

'The Rabbi Loeb is seated at his table in his study with a huge pile of books. He turns the pages, he writes, he opens more books. That is all I see.'

The minister loved hearing this. He could hardly wait for the day to come. What were they all going to eat? Books?

On the day itself, an hour before the banquet was to begin, the Kaiser and the whole court received a request from the Rabbi to come to the great feast. With their coaches and horses and footmen and ladies-in-waiting they arrived, only to find Loeb still poring over his books. The minister could hardly stop himself from jumping up and down.

He looked at Kaiser Rudolf, raised his eyebrows, held

out his hand and was just about to say, 'The man is a liar,' when Loeb said, 'Now let us go to the feast.'

He led the whole group down to the river. There, where there had only been mud and reeds, was a spectacular palace.

'Come in,' said Loeb, 'you are my guests.'

The guests entered and gasped at the splendour of the place. The tables were laid, servants stood ready.

'Please be seated, my friends,' the Rabbi said.

Knives and forks of the finest silver lay alongside dishes of gold and goblets studded with precious jewels. The food was the most exquisite and fragrant that anyone had ever seen.

'Now eat and make merry,' said Loeb, 'but before you start, could I say this? Eat and drink what you like but take nothing else you see before you.'

It was a meal, the like of which none of the people had

ever eaten before. The tastes and flavours mingled in their mouths, startled and delighted the guests' tongues. When it was finished, Rabbi Loeb led his guests into a garden that was laid out with cool fountains, waterfalls, cunning little tunnels and secret springs. There were flowers everywhere; the trees were in blossom and the rich coloured creepers that wound about the bridges were reflected in the streams. There were surprising little nooks among the hedges and some bushes had been trimmed and clipped to grow into fantastic shapes.

When everyone had feasted their bodies and eyes as much as they could, they began to leave. To their surprise, they found the minister who had been so suspicious of the Rabbi, still sitting in his place. He couldn't move. He

just could not leave his seat, but struggled and sweated in his chair. The Kaiser was called in to see.

For a moment he watched the minister and then said to him with a smile, 'I don't think *I* can help you but if you talk to the Rabbi he might be kind enough to do something for you.'

'Rabbi, sir,' said the minister, 'I beg you to set me free.'

'You may remember,' the Rabbi said to all the courtiers crowding round, 'that I did ask that no one should take anything from here. Perhaps someone would be so kind as to look beneath the minister's cloak.'

A courtier stepped up, opened the minister's cloak and pulled out one of the jewel-studded goblets.

'You may go now,' Rabbi Loeb said and the minister muttered into his chest and shuffled off.

The Kaiser now turned to Loeb and said, 'This goblet is beautiful. I've never seen one like it. Perhaps I could buy it.'

'It is not mine to sell,' said Loeb, 'it is only lent to me. But take it and keep it until someone asks for it back.'

'Now do you see?' the Kaiser called out after the minister, 'Rabbi Loeb's a true friend, a man I can trust. You are a fool and a trouble-maker. I'm finished with you, do you hear?'

Of course, the Kaiser and his court were fascinated and puzzled as to how the Rabbi had managed to stage all this, and even more intrigued when by the next day, the palace by the river was gone and all that remained was the same mud and reeds. Some months later, they began to get some idea of what had gone on. A messenger from a far-off land beyond Constantinople, beyond even the Great Ottoman Empire, arrived in Prague. The word soon passed round that a traveller from the East with a story to tell was at the court. An audience collected together, as eager as usual to hear a tale from distant places.

'Our Emperor arranged a wonderful feast for kings, queens, princes and princesses. He had a palace built and filled it with the finest treasures that his craftsmen could make. Believe it or not, one day, the whole palace disappeared. It just disappeared, I tell you, along with all the servants and gardens too. Nobody could understand how it had happened. There was panic and torment for all concerned. Such treasure and beauty lost forever. So many people lost too. There was much wailing and lamenting that night I can tell you. But friends, this disaster didn't last long, because the next day, believe it or not, the new palace was back. The servants couldn't explain where they had been and every single little thing was back the way it was apart from the food and drink and . . . one beautiful goblet. At first everyone was so pleased that friends and relations were back, and the beautiful palace was back. But bit by bit, the Emperor began to be saddened by the loss of this, his favourite goblet. Finally, he could stand it no more, and sent out messengers, north, south, east and west to see see if any of us could find the goblet.'

'Is this the Emperor's goblet?' said the Kaiser.

'Indeed it is,' said the messenger.

So the Kaiser wrapped the goblet in silk, packed a casket with gold and gave it to the messenger from this far-off Emperor. He also wrote a letter apologising for any inconvenience caused by the palace disappearing for a day and explained as best as he could that one of his close friends, a Rabbi, seemed to have extraordinary powers.

CHAPTER SEVEN

The Count

One of the guests at the great banquet was a Count who was another of Thaddeus's friends in high places. This Count was fascinated by astronomy, astrology, magic and mystery. He was desperate to find out how this strange Rabbi had performed these marvels. When he discovered that before the amazing happenings down at the riverside the Rabbi had been poring over old books for weeks, he could hide his curiosity no more. He knew then that the Rabbi was using the Kabbala. You might wonder, what is the Kabbala? The trouble is those who don't know, can't say and those who do know, won't say. People who followed the ways of the Kabbala seemed to live in another world. One moment they would be in a trance and another in a frenzy. They talked of demons and spirits and when they read books it was as if they saw beyond the words on the page to other words. They took things that were written in the Torah and showed how there were always numbers hidden there; numbers of sons of Jacob, numbers of archangels in heaven. Then they took those numbers and wove them into mysterious chants and charms. The books of the Kabbala had strange names like 'The Book of Concealment' or 'The Book of Visions'.

Was Rabbi Loeb really delving into this sort of thing, the Count wondered. He couldn't read Hebrew, the language they were written in, and he was driving himself mad to know more. One night he disguised himself as a beggar and took himself to the Rabbi's house. Once there, he kept watch outside and saw the Rabbi in his study. He watched him moving to and fro, taking books off his shelves, holding the pages up to the candle light, sometimes studying one page for over an hour, other times flicking hurriedly through a whole book. Sometimes he could see the Rabbi's lips moving. What was going on? What was it all about? The Count was wild to know more and could contain himself no more.

The next day he presented himself at the Rabbi's house and rudely invited himself into Loeb's study.

'Now then, Loeb,' said the Count, 'I know what you're up to. You conjured up that palace and the banquet. You sit there grubbing through your old Hebrew books. I'm going to come out with it to your face; you are using the Kabbala. No, don't try to deny it. I'm not here to cause you pain or trouble – though, as you know, there are some people about who would like to see you and all your people drowned in the river, I'm not one of them. I'm after something different. You use the Kabbala. You know it, you follow it and I want you to teach me it. I want it, do you hear me?'

Rabbi Loeb answered, 'I'm afraid it is quite impossible for me to do what you ask. The Kabbala is something that not even many Jews can understand, let alone someone who is not a Jew and cannot read a word of Hebrew.'

'Now listen here, Rabbi,' said the Count, his mouth tightening up, 'I don't care what you think. I don't care if you guess that the likes of me might not be able to grasp all the mysteries of the Kabbala. I order you to teach me, then I can decide for myself if I can use it, thank you very much.'

'My Lord,' said Loeb, 'what I am saying to you is that Jews themselves find it hard to read and learn the ways of the Kabbala. For someone like you who doesn't even know what we do on Friday nights, it would be impossible.'

'Don't you see, Loeb, it is because you say it is impossible that I am driven to want to know. I must, I must, I must be let into the secrets of the Kabbala. I want to work your magic. It can't only be damned Jews who can learn the mysteries. Don't keep putting me off, Loeb,' said the Count.

'I cannot and will not do it,' said the Rabbi, 'and now will you leave my house.'

'You dare stand here in your damp and dirty little study and refuse me? You a Jew, and me a Count? I am a cousin of the Kaiser on his father's side. Don't make me angry, my man. I have power in this city. I have a say over who lives and who dies in Prague, you know. Your life can be snuffed out in a moment and any number of Jews with it. Do you hear me?'

Rabbi Loeb was frightened. 'What you have said and the way you have said it, makes me change my mind. I will try to do what you say, but I beg of you, leave it for a while. I have to send for my teacher, Rabbi Abraham of Saragossa in Spain. If he can come to Prague, he may be able to help me in the difficult, terribly difficult task you have set me.'

'I seem to have hit on something you Jews understand. A little fear and suddenly you find I will be able to understand the secrets of the Kabbala after all. Right, I'll give

you three months to get this Rabbi friend of yours here from Spain, but on that day, three months from now, you will begin the teaching. If not, then you, your wife and dear little children had better watch out. I have wild and hungry soldiers at my command who may not be as learned as you are, but who are well educated in the ideas of Father Thaddeus.'

So saying, the Count swept out of the room.

Loeb sank into his chair. Another trial. Another test. What could he do? What *should* he do?

Perhaps I should write now to Rabbi Abraham, he thought.

But then what will the great man say when he learns that I am asking him to open the secrets of the Kabbala to a Christian – and one who hates Jews at that? And then, what would happen if Rabbi Abraham refused? What terrible things would happen to my family and all the Jews of the city? As his mind roamed over these awful questions, Loeb slumped forward on to his desk and fell asleep.

Suddenly, he felt someone tugging at his sleeve.

'Is that you, Pearl? It's not like me to sleep in the middle of the day, is it? Was I snoring?'

Standing in front of him was a man. Straightaway he saw who it was: his friend and teacher, Rabbi Abraham of Saragossa.

'You need me?' said Abraham.

'How did you get here? cried Rabbi Loeb.

'It's all right,' said Abraham, 'you don't have to tell me a thing. I know and that's why I'm here. My journey has only lasted a few hours. I made use of the "Shem".'

Rabbi Loeb had some idea what Abraham was talking

about. The 'Shem' was a way of saying he had used the secret name of God.

'I will teach the Count,' said Rabbi Abraham, 'don't worry yourself.'

Rabbi Loeb sent a messenger to the Count saying that on the following day the two Rabbis would arrive at his castle; a secret room should be made ready and the teaching of the Kabbala would begin. On the following day, they arrived at the castle and Loeb introduced his friend Abraham to the Count. The Count was already excited by the speed of Rabbi Abraham's coming.

This is a real follower of the Kabbala, he thought. I am about to take on new and magical powers that no other Christian has ever possessed.

'Take us to the secret room,' said Abraham.

'I have prepared a place beneath the castle, in the cellars,' said the Count. He could hardly control his voice.

The three men climbed down stone steps deep into the damp cellars. A long low room was hung with black cloths. Just one candle burnt on a table. The air smelled earthy. The men stopped and stood in silence, the Count not knowing who was going to speak first. No sounds from the outside world reached here; all that could be heard at that moment was the faint sizzle of the candle.

Finally, Abraham spoke, 'Before I begin to show you the secrets of the Kabbala, Count, I must give you this warning: . . .'

The Count breathed in.

'. . . he who wants to look into the books of the Kabbala and possess its secrets has to do so without fear. He who looks into the Kabbala without fear is someone who is not ashamed of anything he has ever done. Only such a man is pure; only such a man can become a follower of the Kabbala. I have to ask you this, Count: are you such a man, a man with no shame of anything you have ever done?'

In a clear, firm voice, the Count said, 'I am.'

'Then turn around just where you are,' said Abraham, 'and LOOK!'

The Count did so, then twisted quickly and violently back again, crying out loud as he did so.

'So you know them?' said Rabbi Abraham.

'Oh my God,' muttered the Count, 'I know them, I know them – my sister and . . . and our child.'

'You, Count, are guilty of the deaths of both of them and you carry that guilt and shame with you. Look at them. See how your sister with your child in her arms gazes at you out of the darkness.'

'I do, I do,' said the Count.

No one spoke.

Finally, after several minutes, the Count turned to the man who knew the secrets he had so longed to know: 'In me, what I have done, cannot be silenced. *You* know, but I order you to be silent and reveal nothing to anyone.'

He turned to Rabbi Loeb: 'I see now that I am not worthy to be taught the ways of the Kabbala. I am sorry for using your time and for threatening you in the way that I did.'

They climbed up the stone steps out of the cellar and, standing together in the high hall, the Count promised Rabbi Loeb that he would never again try to cause him pain or anxiety. For a moment Loeb thought he would ask the Count the favour of banishing Thaddeus from his castle, but in the end chose not, thinking that now he was safe. But then the ways of that strange monk were never really known or understood.

CHAPTER EIGHT

The Dream

Stories of the ways and deeds of Rabbi Loeb were travelling across Europe. In one country, the King passed a law saying that every Jew must leave immediately. Any Jews staying would be put to death and everything they owned would be seized so that it would not pass on to any relative. A party of Jews from this country travelled to Prague to talk with the Rabbi Loeb. When they arrived at his house, they found him in his room, walking up and down, singing an old slow tune. He signalled that they were not to speak and went on singing.

After a short while he spoke to them and said, 'Peace be with you; the matter that is on your minds will be settled by tomorrow.'

That night, far away, the King of that country had a dream. He dreamt he was in his own capital city. It was a hot summer's day and he rode with his servants and favourite courtiers to a forest on the outskirts of the city to bathe in the warm, slow-flowing river there. He dived in, swam across the river, reached the bank on the opposite side and climbed out. There he rested, proud of himself. All at once he found himself watching outraged as his servants and courtiers dressed themselves and hurriedly drove off in the carriages.

He called out to them, 'Come back, come back.'

He waved, he screamed but they seemed not to hear and soon disappeared out of sight. There he stood, naked and cold on the other side of the river, crazed with worry and fear. The best thing to do was to try and find his way home through the forest, so he set off walking without shoes or clothes among the trees. Soon he met a group of woodcutters.

'I am the king,' he said and the men roared out laughing.

'Hey, come over here,' they called out to each other, 'we've got a right one here, haven't we? Wandering about the forest, stark naked, saying he's the king. That's right, mate, and I'm God and my friend here is Jesus Christ.'

And they began to poke and push at the king.

'Careful you don't get cold, my Lord,' said one, 'bits of you could drop off in this weather, and who knows what bits? Eh? Eh?'

One of the woodcutters slapped his bare backside so hard the sound seemed to smack the trees around. The woodcutter's handprint showed up on the king's left buttock.

'That's so you don't get lost, my Lord,' says he, 'you'll be able to tell which is top and which is bottom now.'

Again, the woodcutters fell about laughing. After a while they got bored and the King was able to get away from them. He ran and ran till his feet were bleeding and he was gasping for air. He roamed around in the forest like a stray goat till he met up with an old beggar. The beggar gave him a few tatty torn clothes from out of his bag and led him slowly back to the city.

48

As soon as he started coming across people in the street he tried to talk to them.

'I am the king, I am the king,' he called out.

People turned away, as people do, when they see a man or a woman in old clothes shouting out strange things in the street. Children ran away and watched him from behind pillars and drinking fountains.

So the beggar-king wandered through the city, and then from town to town until eventually he left his own country and wandered across several others. At last, he arrived at the city of Prague, where by chance, he wandered into the Jewish ghetto.

Seeing poor Jews in the street and thinking of the Bible, he said to himself, 'These people are like me, or I am like them. Once they were proud and great and now they are poor and afraid. See what they have been brought down to!'

He started talking with some Jews in the market-place and told them who he was and what had happened to him.

One man said, 'You should meet our Rabbi, Rabbi Loeb, he might have some advice to give you. What has happened to you, shouldn't happen to a dog.'

He led the beggar to Loeb who greeted him as a King even though he stood dirty and battered in old tatty clothes.

'My Lord,' said Loeb, 'a man who looks like you, sounds like you, and moves like you has become the King of your country in your place. No one knows that he is not you. As it happens, he is, this very day, here in Prague and is due to go down to the river to bathe. When he is in the water, why don't you do to him what was done to you?'

Rabbi Loeb found a hairdresser and a tailor, and between them they cleaned up the king, trimmed his nails, oiled his skin, and brought him back to the way he once looked.

'Now,' said Rabbi Loeb, 'if you wish to become King of your country once more, just sign this document, will you? And the copy too. There's no need to read all of it. It simply says that I, the King, wish to cancel the law I made that banished the Jews from my country. That law is no more.'

The King signed and then took himself down to the river. He waited for the false King to get into the water, then quickly stole his clothes and drove off in the royal carriage . . . but there the dream finished. He woke up in his own bed.

Glancing around him, he saw something on his bedside table. It was the copy of the paper he had signed in his dream. He was about to blurt out, 'Unbelievable!', when he was even more staggered to see there, on the table, next to the paper was a tray. On the tray, was a little heap of dirty hair, beard trimmings and disgusting bits of filthy fingernails.

The Jews were not thrown out of the country. Rabbi Loeb had once again used his powers to keep people safe from disaster and terror. Of course, the Jews of Prague were proud and pleased he had done so, but some wondered, could he be so clever if such a disaster, God forbid, threatened *them*? Weren't there still dangerous people and fearsome spirits at loose in the city?

CHAPTER NINE

The Golem

Thaddeus, friend of the people stood in his pulpit on Sundays and railed against the Jews.

'People of Prague, listen before it is too late. The Jews' synagogues must be set on fire and whatever is left buried in dirt so that no one may ever be able to see a stone or cinder of it. Their prayer books must be burnt and their Rabbis must be forbidden to preach. Jews' homes must be smashed and destroyed and the Jews flung into stables, like Gypsies, to teach them they are not masters in our land. They must be banned from the roads and markets, their property seized. And then these poisonous worms must be forced to work to earn their bread by the sweat of their noses. Since we break highwaymen, murderers and housebreakers on the wheel and then behead them, so must we break all Jews on the wheel – hunt down, kill and behead them all.'

Out of sight he made plans. He was trying to find some way in which he could take the Jews to court and find them guilty of killing Christians. And then, he hoped that his people on hearing what Jews had done, would flock to the ghetto to burn, loot and murder. Every day, news came to Loeb that people were being stirred up. The safety of every Jew was in danger.

The Rabbi sat and thought: why is this happening? No nation has the right to rule over another. Don't we learn from the time we are young that for the sake of peace among all people, we trace back all humankind to one person, Adam, so that no man may say to his neighbour, 'My father is better than yours.' But now we are faced with destruction. The Kaiser says he is not against us, the Cardinal says he is not against us and yet we could all be wiped out. What is to be done?

Loeb fell asleep as he pondered and as he slept he dreamt. In his dream came the words, 'Ato bra Golem Devuk Hakhomer V'tigzar Zedim Chevek Torfe Yisroel.'

What did it mean?

'Make a Golem out of clay and you will destroy all those who threaten the Jews.'

Loeb woke up. A Golem? What is this Golem? He knew the word meant 'a living body without a soul'. Adam was a Golem before God breathed life and soul into him. But how could he, Loeb, make a living body, a Golem? In an old book he read, once, long ago, two magical men studied and learnt how to make a live calf. On the eve of Sabbath every week they made a calf that ate and drank and ran about. But when the men killed it and ate the meat, they forgot all they had learnt and spent the rest of the week learning how to make the calf again. As he read deeper and deeper into the books, Loeb began to get some idea of how he might create a Golem. He followed closely what it said in one book especially, the 'Sefer Yezirah' – 'The Book of Creation' – and then he called for his daughter's husband, Isaac ben Simson and his favourite pupil, Jacob ben Chayim Sasson.

They gathered in Loeb's study and the Rabbi told them of his dream and his studies.

'To save us from all those who threaten us, I shall try to make this Golem. To do this I need the four elements: "Aysch" – fire, "Mayim" – water, "Ruach" – air and "Aphar" – earth. You, Isaac, are the element of fire, you, Jacob, are water, I am air. Together we shall take the fourth element, earth, and make a Golem.'

On the second day of the month of Adar, after midnight, the men took themselves to the ritual baths. They sang and prayed, Loeb read over the 'Book of Creation' one more time and then all three, with the synagogue servant along to help, went on to the outskirts of the city, down to the riverside where Loeb had conjured up the palace.

They lit torches and sang psalms from the Torah into the night air. Then they began to dig in the sticky mud, heaping up a fair-sized tump. Now Loeb started moulding the heap into the shape of a huge human figure. He pushed and pulled at the mud till there, by the side of the river lay a giant mud man, staring up at the night sky.

Loeb said, 'Isaac, walk seven times round the thing. Walk from its right hand to its left, round its head. As you walk, say these "Zifurim" charms.'

And Loeb told him the secret words to say. As Isaac came round for the seventh and last time the mud figure began to glow red in the dark like coal in a fire.

'Jacob, walk the other way, from left to right, round its head. Say these "Zifurim" . . .'

And he told Jacob more secret words. As Jacob came round for the seventh time, the red glow faded but suddenly hair began to grow on the figure's body and head; nails appeared on the fingers and toes; water flowed through its body. Then Rabbi Loeb himself walked once around it. He placed in its mouth a tiny piece of parchment with the 'Shem', the secret name of God, written on it. He took up a stick and marked its forehead with 'Emet' which means Truth.

He bowed to the east, the west, the south and the north and then all three men said together the part of the Torah where God created Adam, 'And He breathed into his nostrils the breath of life, and man became a living being.'

Loeb had made a Golem.

It opened its eyes and looked around with a face that looked as if it could see everything but understand nothing.

'Stand up,' said Rabbi Loeb.

The Golem stood up, towering above them. The others looked on terrified. Loeb told them to help him dress it in the clothes of a 'shammes', the man who looks after and prepares everything in the synagogue. They pushed and squeezed its arms and legs into the sleeves and folds of the clothes, yet it just stood loose, letting them do it.

The Rabbi spoke out loudly and clearly in the dark to the Golem: 'Know these things: we have made you from the earth. It will be your task to protect Jews. You will be called Joseph and you will live in my house. You, Joseph, must do what I say, no matter where I send you: through fire and water, if I command you to jump from a housetop or if I send you to the bottom of the sea.'

Joseph nodded.

'You will not be able to speak. You are not good or bad. You are like a pump or a mill that obeys whoever has made you. No law governs you. You do not long for women and the love of women. You will never be ill, you will never be evil. You do not know about God but you can see all hidden things. On the Day of Judgement, on the last day of the earth, you will be there but in what shape we do not know. That is all. Now we shall go home.'

The men and the Golem slowly made their way back to the ghetto and the Rabbi's house. In the morning, Loeb explained to his family and friends that he had been called out in the night because a huge stranger who couldn't speak was wandering in the street.

'I felt sorry for him,' he said. 'I am taking him on as

an extra shammes in the synagogue. I shall call him
Joseph. No one, but no one, must ever send Joseph off to
do things: shopping, cleaning, lifting or anything like it.
No one. He must only be asked to do things in the service
of our religion.'

Amazed and curious, people agreed to what the Rabbi
said. Everyone had learnt by now not to question too
closely the ways of this strange and magical man.

CHAPTER TEN

The Fish and the Apples

In the Rabbi's house lived a poor orphan girl whom the Loebs had taken in and treated as their own daughter. She was to be married and the Rabbi and his wife acted as her parents, preparing a wedding feast for her and her man and inviting guests. Pearl was busier than she had ever been: preparing the food, polishing the silver, running to and fro.

'Up to my eyes with this, I am. It'll never be finished.'

Suddenly she discovered she was short of fish. As she stood there wondering what to do, the woman who helped her in the kitchen came in and said they were short of apples.

'Have I got "tsirres"! Have I got trouble! First I find that I've hardly got enough fish to feed a sparrow, and now she's telling me here that I haven't got enough apples to make the "strudel".'

Pearl could see that everyone else was busy about the house, except for the newcomer, this silent giant of a chap, Joseph.

All day he just sits, thought Pearl. Maybe I could send him to get me fish and apples? But then should I? Didn't Judah Loeb say he must only be used in the service of our religion? But then aren't I doing a good deed, a 'mitzvah' by marrying off this poor orphan girl to someone who's done very well for himself? Perhaps it would be all right if I sent him off to help this mitzvah. That would be, as Judah said, 'in the service of our religion', wouldn't it? Please God, nothing should happen.

She called the Golem over.

'Joseph, do you hear me?'

He nodded.

'Go to the River Market and bring from the fisherman some fish. When you've come back from there, go to the Street Market and bring back best apples.'

She gave Joseph two pieces of paper, one for the fisherman and one for the fruit-seller, asking them to give the fish and apples to the big silent fellow. Joseph went to the fisherman and collected a live carp weighing twenty nine pounds. He didn't wait for a bag but stuffed it down his shirt, head down with the tail sticking up in front of his face. It seemed as good a place as any to put it, but on the way home, the fish wriggled and then smacked Joseph right across the face with its tail. It hit him so hard that he staggered across the street. He was furious.

Rightaway, he turned around where he was and headed back for the river. When he got there, he ripped the carp out of his shirt and flung it in with all the strength he had. It flew down to the water with such force, it sank to the bottom. All this before the fisherman could stop him.

When he got back, Pearl asked him for the fish.

'Quick Joseph, the carp, give it here.'

Joseph stood there for a moment and then acted out what had happened, waving his arms around and jumping up and down. People stopped rushing about to watch.

They all thought it was a great joke. Well, all except for Pearl, who was now short of fish for the wedding. She shook her head in despair. Wasn't being without enough food to give people at a wedding more shameful than lying or cheating even?

Before she could do anything about it, the Golem was off again, this time to the Street Market. The fruit-seller weighed out the apples and asked him if he wanted a bag. Joseph showed her that he could carry them in his arms. The fruit-woman laughed, at which Joseph flew into a rage, grabbed hold of the woman, the apples, the weighing scales, the baskets and the stall itself; heaved it all on to his thick shoulders and marched off through the city.

The woman screamed at Joseph, 'Put me down, you "meshuggener"! Put me down, madman!'

People ran to see what was happening and saw this strange huge man rushing through the streets with a fruit-seller on his shoulders and hundreds of apples in his arms. No one dared stop him.

When he reached the Loebs' house, he banged on the door for Pearl to come and see. In a blink of an eye he put the stall together, put the scales, the baskets the apples in place and then stood the woman behind the stall. A huge crowd gathered round, not knowing whether to laugh or run away at these wild goings on. Through the window of his study, Rabbi Loeb looked up and saw what was happening. In the middle of the crowd, stood the Golem.

'Joseph, come to me,' called out Loeb.

The Golem came running and then once again waving his arms and jumping about showed the Rabbi what had happened.

The Rabbi laughed at the sight of it.

'I thought one big occasion was enough for one day, what with the wedding of our girl. You've brought here enough people for another wedding with all this "shemozzle" and carry-on.'

For years after, if someone lost their temper and started doing crazy things people in Prague would say, 'Fish and apples to you. Fish and apples!'

CHAPTER ELEVEN

The Water

Rabbi Loeb knew there were serious matters ahead for Joseph the Golem but everyday life has to go on. Food has to be fetched, houses have to be cleaned, faces have to be washed.

Pearl, seeing Joseph sitting on a barrel in the corner of the kitchen called out to him, 'Hey, lift a hand to help round here. Fetch some water from the river, will you?'

Off went Joseph with the buckets, off went Pearl to do the shopping. When she got back, the house was flooded. There was water everywhere. People were shouting and dashing in and out. Next moment, Joseph appeared round the corner with his buckets, reached the yard, tipped up the buckets and marched off again. 'Stop, stop,' shouted Pearl but he took no notice. 'What's happening here? It looks like the Flood but no Noah to build us an ark. He'll wash us all away, the way he is going. What are we going to do?'

Joseph wasn't bothered. Soon he was back with more water. He hurled it into the house. The cellar was full, jars and baskets were floating out into the kitchen. The back yard was awash. Any moment now, it would reach the Rabbi's study and the thousands of precious books would be ruined.

'Stop, for God's sake stop!' shouted Pearl and everyone else joined in.

Joseph took not the slightest bit of notice and hurried on doing just as he was told to do: fetching water from the river.

Shortly after, Rabbi Loeb was back from the synagogue. He quickly took in what was happening. When Joseph came back with yet another water-load there was panic. Pearl rushed up to him and tried to grab the buckets off him, but the Golem just pushed her out of his way.

Loeb knew that Joseph had been asked to do something that had nothing to do with religion. Nothing that anyone said to him would get him to stop.

Perhaps even I might not be able to stop this madness, said the Rabbi to himself.

He stepped towards the Golem, 'Enough water now, Joseph.'

The Golem made to fling the buckets of water yet again, but hesitated, then stopped. The madness had come to an end.

This time it has worked, thought Loeb, another time I may not be so lucky.

'Listen,' he said to everybody. 'I meant what I said: no one must ask Joseph to do something that is not part of our religion.'

Everyone was left to clear up the mess and from that time they looked at Joseph differently. They had seen him doing crazy things in such a serious way and they knew that none of them had the power to stop him. It was frightening, they said. Like a demon, he was. No one gave him work like that to do again.

As with the fish and apples, people spoke of it years later.

If, say, a carpenter was doing a bad job but wouldn't listen to what other people were saying about it, people would say, 'You make chairs like that Joseph carries water!'

CHAPTER TWELVE

The Dead Girl

It was coming up to Passover and Rabbi Loeb found himself getting worried that people who had been mixing with Thaddeus would be up to their tricks again. He took the Golem on one side: 'Joseph, every night, I want you to wander the streets of the ghetto, looking out for anyone doing what they shouldn't be doing. Look for people with strange bundles. Look for people trying to leave things in people's houses. Watch and look, Joseph.'

So, every night, Joseph went out of the house and roamed the streets of the ghetto looking about him, hiding in doorways and watching.

At this time, there lived in Prague a rich and famous Jewish fur-trader called Moredecai Meisel. One of the people he traded with was called Havlicek and though Meisel didn't know it, Havlicek was a friend of Thaddeus. He was a butcher by trade and coming up to this Passover, he owed Meisel five thousand gulden – a lot of money. There was no way that Havlicek would be able to get the money to pay Meisel.

'If only there was some way I could get rid of Meisel,

then all my troubles would be over,' said Havlicek to himself.

He talked to Thaddeus and they hatched a plan. Havlicek had to find the dead body of a Christian child and smuggle it into the house of Mordecai Meisel and then, that night, rush to the police and tell them that he knew that Meisel had something to do with the murder of a child.

Two nights before Passover, Havlicek went out to the cemetery. In the dark, with not so much as a candle to light his work, he dug into a new grave. He soon got down to the coffin and levered open the lid. Inside was the body of a young girl who had died of pneumonia. He lifted her out, closed the coffin, shovelled back the earth and then hurried back to his butcher's shop with the body in his bag. Once there, he took his butcher's knife and cut two lines in the girl's throat, to try and make it look like the cuts Jewish butchers make on whatever animal their customers eat. He then wrapped the girl in a Jewish prayer shawl and put the body inside the carcass of a dead pig – an animal that Jews don't eat. He thought that all this would make it look as if it were part of some kind of weird Jewish ceremony.

Havlicek went out once more into the night. He put the pig, with the girl's corpse inside, on to his waggon and, as quietly as he could, he drove towards the ghetto. Now, in the dead of night, very slowly and quietly, he drew near to Meisel's house; found the trap door to his cellar, and got ready to hurl the bundle down through the door. Just then, Joseph loomed out of the shadows.

There was a waggon. There was a man. There was a bundle. Wasn't that just the sort of thing that the Rabbi had told him to look out for? Faster than you can blink, he was at Havlicek's side. He grabbed the bundle, ripped off the cover and saw the pig. He flung it back into the waggon and then lifted Havlicek up on to the driving seat. Before he could think, Joseph tied him up with the rope from the bundle. Havlicek was no weakling. He spent much of his day, heaving huge animal carcasses to and fro, but try as he could, he couldn't release himself from the grip of the rope. Now Joseph leapt up on to the driving seat beside him and, pulling on the reins, drove off to the house of the city judge. Havlicek struggled and swore under his breath but he couldn't budge. He knew he was a prisoner and the guard that had captured him was stronger than any man he had ever seen before. He had tree trunks for arms and his back was like a door. Helpless, Havlicek sat on his waggon praying for someone or something to release him from this massive speechless man.

At the judge's house, Joseph banged on the door and roused the sheriff and several officers, as well as the judge himself. They tumbled out on to the street, with torches burning to see the strange spectacle of the big butcher tied up on the seat of his own waggon, the even bigger silent man beside him and a dead pig behind them. In a few minutes they found out that things were even stranger. There was a girl's dead body there, too.

Havlicek knew he could deny nothing; 'Yes I did all this. I admit it. You don't know what it's like to owe money to a Jew. That Meisel's got plenty. All right, so I owe him money, but I can't pay yet. But you can never get a few more days to pay back a Jew, can you? I thought if you found this stuff in his cellar it would put him inside for a while. I thought he might even hang for it and I could sleep in peace.'

The judge didn't waste time. 'Put him in the cell and we'll deal with him in the morning. Now where's that other fellow? The big one who didn't have a word to say.'

No one knew. One moment he had been there and the next he was gone.

69

In the morning when the story spread through the city, people tried to make sense of the whole affair. Loeb, knowing that Joseph was doing the work he had set him, was secretly delighted. Elsewhere in the city, Thaddeus was furious, but at the same time mystified. How come the silent giant had caught Havlicek? How did he know what Havlicek had been up to?

That Loeb is behind this, he thought, and so next time he spoke from his pulpit, the people's friend reached out to his flock saying, 'I warn you, oh my people, amongst these Jews lives someone who looks like a man, talks like a man but is really the devil himself. He is a sorcerer, a man-witch. He has a giant as a slave and will work his evil magic on us all. We must strike before his magic strikes us or we are all doomed. God threw the devil out of His kingdom to show us that we must do the same on earth. My people, the devil must be chased from here and never seen again.'

CHAPTER THIRTEEN

The Poison

Passover came and the Rabbi was in the 'Altneuschul', the Old-New Synagogue, saying the prayers. Suddenly, he heard himself making a mistake. Instead of saying in the prayer, 'He changes the seasons' – 'unmachalif es hazmanim', he said, 'He turns the seasons sour' – 'unmachamitz es hazmanim'. Loeb stopped speaking right in the middle of the prayer.

What does this mean? Perhaps it is telling me that somewhere, someone is planning an attack on our people. 'I must stop the prayers now,' he said.

He spoke to the people in the synagogue. 'You must go on with the prayers yourselves, but no one, no one at all can leave here until I say so.'

He turned to the old shammes, Abraham, and told him to go to every other synagogue in Prague and say that Loeb ordered everyone not to leave until they heard again later from him telling them they could go. Off went Abraham, and the Rabbi called for the Golem.

'Joseph, go quickly to our house and bring me some matzos: bring me one piece of the matzo we eat every day and one piece of "matzo shel mitzvah", special Passover matzo.'

71

In a few minutes, Joseph was back.

'Now Joseph,' said the Rabbi, 'eat this ordinary matzo.'

Joseph put it in his mouth, rubbed his belly and nodded. He liked it and held out his hand for more.

'And now, Joseph, eat the "matzo shel mitzvah".'

Joseph bit into it happily, but a few seconds later, grabbed his throat and began to squirm around in pain. A moment later he was holding his belly and writhing about. He fell on the floor, his face twisted up. The whole synagogue watched in fear.

The Golem looked up at Loeb, his face a mixture of pain, terror and even anger. His eyes seemed to be saying, why have you done this to me? Why are you hurting me like this? The Rabbi saw the look, knelt down and passed his hand over the Golem's body. Straightaway, Joseph stopped twisting, the pain passed from his face and he stood up smiling and nodding.

Immediately, the Rabbi was surrounded with people asking him questions: 'What does this mean? What is going on? Where did you get this matzo from?'

'Don't worry, don't worry,' said Loeb. 'What you have seen, is all that I have seen. We have to believe we won't be destroyed. If we help ourselves now we can save ourselves.'

He called on one of his followers to hurry after Abraham the shammes to all the synagogues of Prague with a new message: 'Rabbi Loeb says that all the Passover matzos baked in Prague must not be eaten, because they are "chometz", not proper Passover matzos. No one must touch the matzos. No child must be allowed to nibble the tiniest bit, or pick up even the smallest crumb. Better to go hungry than eat these matzos. It's a matter of life and death.'

Now the Rabbi began his investigation. He went down to the matzo bakery to talk to everyone who worked there. Everyone he saw, he knew.

'Listen friends,' he said, 'have any of you seen anything strange, anyone you don't know hanging about the bakery? Has anyone who doesn't normally work here been in?'

One of the bakery workers spoke up. 'Yesterday, we were so hard pressed, Rabbi, we didn't think we'd have enough matzos to go round. So what do we do? We take on two fellows to help with the "rodling", making the lines across the matzo. Now I think of it I'm not sure I know their names. We just called them "The Red-beards".'

Loeb turned to Abraham the shammes and said, 'Tell all the people waiting in the synagogues that only the matzo baked yesterday is "chometz" and cannot be eaten. All the rest is fine and should be shared out amongst us all. Let those who have plenty give to those who have little or none. Everyone should go home, enjoy Seder Night, "gut yomtov", have a good holiday.'

Abraham took the Rabbi's ring to show everyone that he came straight from Loeb.

Loeb himself made his way home, thinking carefully about what he now knew of this business. He needed help.

'Joseph!' he called and the Golem was at his side. 'I want you to go to the house of the two Red-beards who worked at the matzo bakery yesterday. You must not be seen by anyone. I want you to search their house. If you find any little bottle of liquid, any little jar or box, any little packet of powder, bring such a thing back to me here. And remember, no one must see you.'

Off went the Golem. When he got to the house, neither

of the Red-beards was at home. Joseph slipped quietly into the house, and paced about looking. Very soon, he came across a little hard-wood box of powder tucked behind the stove. He took it back to Loeb.

The Rabbi smelt it. 'Same smell as the Passover matzo, the "matzo shel mitzvah".' He handed the little box back to the Golem. 'Now Joseph, go back to the Red-beards' house and put this box of powder exactly where you found it. And remember you must not be seen.'

Next, Loeb called for Abraham the shammes and the two of them made their way to the police.

On the way, who should they meet but the two Red-beards who called out in their thin voices, 'Gut yomtov', have a nice holiday. Though they weren't Jews they had spent enough time with them to know their sayings and ways. They thought it made it easier for them to mix with Jews. Loeb and Abraham walked on down the street. The Red-beards stopped and turned their pale faces to watch Loeb and Abraham as they hurried to the police.

At the police office, they listened to Loeb's story and two men were sent off to the Red-beards' house. They found the little hard-wood box of powder behind the stove and immediately ordered a search to be made for the men themselves. They were found lingering around the edge of the ghetto kicking stones and they were brought before the police. The two men wouldn't say a thing. They just turned their pale faces to the ground and stared.

'Can you explain why you have this box of powder in your house? And why does some of it seem to be missing?'

Nothing: the Red-beards wouldn't say a word.

'If you tell the truth your punishment will be mild. If you lie, or say nothing, you may be hanged for attempted murder.'

They wound and unwound fingers and thumbs. They behaved like two men sharing one bellyache.

Finally, one of them spoke up. 'Yes, look, we go into Jews' homes. I've no complaints.'

'Well?'

'Some time ago, a monk called Thaddeus sent for us. He said, "The Jews like you. It won't be long before they'll want to take you on as some of their servants." He told us that we would be lost souls. We would be in the clutches of the devil himself. He told us about what they do at Passover with Christian children. So we said we wouldn't work for them. But then he switched horses and said no, we must go and work for them because we could watch what they do. It was our duty. We would be spies for God and a place in heaven would be ours.'

'What's this got to do with the poison?'

'I'm coming to that. We told him things the Jews did. He wanted us to tell him about how they kill the animals they eat. He always wanted to know what they did with the blood. It was always the blood he wanted to know about. One day he gave us a little bottle of liquid and told us to get in with Berger the wine-seller. Then when the time was right we were to pour a few drops of it into his barrels. He said we were the Lord's soldiers and our souls would be blessed forever more.

'We weren't allowed anywhere near the wine, and we told him. So the next time we see him, he's getting excited. He tells us he doesn't believe we're really trying to obey the word of the Lord and anyone who is not with God is against God. He said we were doing devil's work and we would burn in hell forever and ever. He kept saying that the Jews were plotting day and night to destroy us all and only we could stop them. One moment he was threatening us and the next he was begging. He put his hands on our heads and called us his sons and said that this Passover was the last chance the good people of Prague would have to save themselves. This time he told us to get taken on at the matzo bakery. He knew that every Jew has to eat special matzo, so he gave us the powder to put in the flour. "This way," he said, "we will be rid of them all. This will be *their* Last Supper, so help me God".'

The Red-beard stopped talking.

'So what did you do with the powder?'

'We get on well with Jews, I've no complaints, really I haven't. We got jobs at the bakery. It was no trouble. There came a time when no one was around and we tipped the powder into the dough. There's a place in heaven for us, he said. All we had to do was take it. It was there waiting for us. What else could we do? I only had to look into the bread ovens to see the fires of hell burning us forever after. Lord save us. We did what was right.'

All this was taken down in writing, the Passover matzos were sent off to be tried out on some rats. They died instantly. Then Thaddeus was sent for. Fresh as ever, bustling with energy and goodwill, he bounced up the steps to the office.

'Do you know these men?' said the police, pointing to the Red-beards. Thaddeus looked into their faces with an interested, kindly look on his face. His eyes moved from one to the other searching for some part that might look familiar.

'I can say with my hand on my heart, I have never seen them before in my life.'

'Have you ever had in your possession any bottles or boxes of poison?'

'On my oath before God, I can say never. You may search my house from top to bottom and you will never find such material. Gentlemen, I would like to be of as much use to this office as I can. Like you, I am on earth to serve the people of Prague. If these men are part of some wrong-doing, then they must be punished. I am of course only too happy to hear their confessions or administer the Last Rites if they are to be hanged for what they have done.'

With talk like this there was nothing more to be said. Thaddeus was thanked and dismissed. When the Redbeards came up in court, not one word did they mention of a monk called Thaddeus. They were sent to prison for five years. Only one of them lived the full length of the sentence. The other died cursing the name of Thaddeus.

Rabbi Loeb was left thinking about the mistake he had made while saying the prayers. 'What a miracle that I said "unmachamitz" instead of "unmachalif". I said "turns sour" instead of "changes". What a miracle!'

CHAPTER FOURTEEN

The Runaways

Another year passed and all seemed to be going well. Once again, Passover was drawing near. Just before the holiday, a little piece of news spread through the ghetto:

'You know Dinah, the doctor's daughter? She's left home.'

'Left home? Don't tell me: she found a young man.'

'No. She wants to be a "goy", a Christian. She's gone, away into Prague.'

'Funny you should say. I always knew there was something odd about that girl. I always knew . . .'

Next day, another piece of news visited the ghetto streets: 'You know Yana the Christian girl who worked at Goldfarb's house on the Sabbath, the "shabbes goya"?'

'Don't tell me: she's stolen a gold ring. I know already.'

'No. She says she got fed up with the Goldfarbs and she's gone home.'

'Well, what I heard was that the Goldfarbs are fed up with her. They say she stole a beautiful gold ring of theirs.'

So two little pieces of news about two runaway girls, Dinah and Yana, nothing to do with each other, floated about the ghetto on people's lips for a day or two and then slipped away with the wind. But elsewhere, someone thought long and hard about them. Thaddeus wondered how he could make something of it. How could he achieve what he had so far failed to do?

He took one of his followers on one side. 'I want you to find Yana Capek, the Jew Goldfarb's servant. She'll be at home by now. Take her somewhere far into the country and hide her.'

To another he said. 'I want you to find Dinah Maridi, a Jewish woman who has escaped from the ghetto. We must have her here before she goes to the Cardinal about becoming a Christian.'

Thaddeus's servants did both these tasks, hiding Yana, no one knows where and bringing Dinah to meet Thaddeus himself. No one quite knows what he said to her but the next week, when she went before the Cardinal, she had a lot to say.

'Your holiness, I wish to become a Christian.'

'Young woman,' said the Cardinal, 'why do you wish to change your religion?'

'I am disgusted by the foul and horrible things Jews do. Their ceremonies make me sick. How can anyone stay with a religion that year in year out kills a Christian child at Passover time to put their blood in the Passover matzos?'

'I would like to ask you one question, young woman,' said the Cardinal. 'How do you know that the Jews kill Christian children?'

'Your holiness,' said Dinah, 'a few days before Passover, there came to my father, two of the Rabbi's servants. One was old and short, the other was a huge giant of a man who couldn't speak. The old man said, "The Rabbi brings you this little bottle of Christian blood for Passover." My father handed the man many gold pieces and ordered my mother to mix the blood with the matzo balls for the soup on Seder Night. When I saw this I made up my mind to give up this horrible cursed people and come and find hope and peace with people such as yourself, your holiness.'

'How do you think the Jews find Christian children to kill for this purpose? As far as I know, young lady, there is no one missing just now.'

'Your holiness, I don't know what you know. All I know is something I've overheard. I heard the Rabbi's servant talking to some people called the Goldfarbs. He said, "Yana is with us no more – but don't worry! When summer comes you will have a new "shabbes goya", a new servant, God willing." What do you think, "with us no more" means, your holiness?'

'Thank you for telling me all this,' said the Cardinal. 'You may go. We will discuss your conversion to Christianity at a later date.'

The Cardinal now did two things. The first was what he had to do: to inform the police of what Dinah had told him. The second he did secretly: he sent a letter to Rabbi Loeb telling him of everything Dinah had said.

'I don't believe a word of what this Dinah says,' he wrote. 'Can I urge you to follow up every thread of her story or it will ruin us all.'

Loeb read the letter through. First thing that'll happen, he thought, is that the police will come for this old and short servant Dinah talked about – that's Abraham the shammes, and they'll come for the giant who can't speak as well. That's Joseph the Golem, of course. Just as a guess, I would think that Dinah never saw Joseph. She's just heard about him from Thaddeus. He only knows

81

about Joseph from when Joseph tied up Havlicek the butcher on his waggon.

Rabbi Loeb sent for his old friend Reuben, a huge man, an actor and something of a show-off. 'Reuben, if you want to save us all, help me now. I want you to pretend you cannot speak, you understand me? For everything you want or need, you have to make signs. I want you to sleep where my servant Joseph sleeps. At some time during the night, anything might happen. I can say no more.'

Reuben agreed, and later lay down in Joseph's bed and went to sleep, while Joseph himself was hidden in the cellar.

At just before midnight, police officers came to Abraham the shammes's house, seized him and put him in chains. They went on to the Rabbi's house.

'We have reason to believe that a man in your house has been involved in a crime. He has been reported to us as being very large and unable to speak. Do you have such a man in your house, sir?'

Rabbi Loeb took them to Reuben and they led him off in chains, too.

At any time now, Loeb thought, they could come back for me. The moment I go, then any effort to find Yana, the shabbes goya, the girl who used to work for the Goldfarbs, will come to an end. Rabbi Loeb found himself beginning to panic. Everything had happened so quickly and he could see in his mind's eye how in court everything would look so clear: Dinah will say that we kill Christian children. Yana, the shabbes goya has disappeared, they will say we killed her and before we know it, mobs will be at the ghetto gates crying for murder and revenge.

The trial was to happen in two days' time. He had just

two days to find some way out of this fix.

He called for Joseph. 'Do you remember Yana, the shabbes goya who used to work for the Goldfarbs on the Sabbath?'

Joseph nodded.

'I want you to find her. Look for her in Prague. Look for her in the countryside in all the villages outside Prague. You have to hurry. You *must* find her or we will all die. When you see her, give her this letter.'

Loeb didn't know she had been hidden by Thaddeus's servants. All he knew was that she had to be found.

The letter that Joseph took was made out to look as if it had come from the Goldfarbs, like this:

Dear Yana

The ring that was lost has been found. I beg your pardon a thousand times for having said that you took it. You were very honest with me, but I was unfair to you. I beg you, the moment that you see this letter to come back to Prague with the man who has brought it to you. The children, especially little Sarah, miss you very much and are looking forward to your coming back. We all know how much we like you and need you. We are sending you twenty-five gulden for the money you must have spent on travel.

Love and God bless
Rachel Goldfarb

The Goldfarbs knew nothing of this letter.

Then off went Joseph the Golem. A whole day passed with no sign of him or Yana. It seemed to Loeb that at last, Thaddeus had got the better of them and a terrible

83

day was about to arrive. He thought of all those other cities in Europe where troops had suddenly arrived at ghetto walls and thousands of Jews had been murdered. The day of the trial came and still no Joseph, no Yana.

At the courthouse, a great crowd of people had gathered. The street was full. When Thaddeus arrived, fresh-faced and serious, they cheered and shouted, 'God bless you, Father. God bless Thaddeus,' and they pressed forward to touch him. When Loeb arrived, there were boos and screams, 'Murderer! Sorcerer!'

He hurried into the court as people crowded round and hurled old apples and woody turnips at him. Inside, the trial began.

'You, Abraham Chayim, Rabbi Loeb's servant, and you the unnamed servant of the same Rabbi Loeb are accused of having murdered Yana Capek the sabbath servant at the household of the Goldfarbs. Did you, Abraham Chayim take Christian blood to Jews' houses before Passover?'

'No,' said Abraham.

The judge held up some little bottles full of red liquid. 'Have you ever carried bottles like this?' he said to the silent man.

Reuben was in a difficult situation. He had to pretend not to know what was going on, but at the same time he didn't actually know anyway. He raised his eyebrows, smiled and nodded keenly, then poked his finger towards his mouth.

'The man cannot hear,' said Abraham and Reuben's lawyer, Levy.

Thaddeus leapt to his feet. 'My Lord, it is quite clear. The man is saying that he has carried a little bottle like that and he pokes his finger in his mouth to show us that people have put whatever is in the bottle into their food and eaten it.'

A great cheer went up from the crowd.

Levy stepped forward. 'The man thinks the bottle contains wine and he thinks you're asking him if he wants to drink it. So he nods. What else would he do?'

Levy took a knife, pointed to Loeb and then to the bottle. He was trying to ask Reuben if he knew anything about a murder, the Rabbi and the bottle. Reuben now trembled and shook his head over and over again, looking very scared.

Thaddeus leapt to his feet again. 'The man thinks you are asking him if Loeb should be killed, so he is saying no, of course.'

'Order! Order!' shouted the judge. 'Call Dinah Maridi.'

Dinah first told the story about the shammes coming with the little bottle of blood to her parents' house, followed by what she said she had heard at the Goldfarbs about Yana and a new shabbes goya.

Levy asked her, 'Do you know the Rabbi's servants well? The ones who came to your father with the little bottles of blood?'

'I know them well,' said Dinah. 'There they are. I would know them in a cellar on a dark night.'

'My Lord,' said Levy, 'may we call Dinah Maridi's mother and father. We need to know whether they agree with Dinah that they saw the Rabbi's servants and this bottle.'

Thaddeus was on his feet again. 'My Lord, we have a witness, Dinah, we have the murderers. Can we move on? There is no point in wasting time with parents and relations. A fine young Christian girl is dead, my Lord.'

'Hang them!' shouted the crowd.

The judge wavered. He began to be swayed by the mood in the court.

He turned to Levy, 'Do you have anything further to say?'

Levy looked around him helplessly. He didn't. He glanced across to Rabbi Loeb. Loeb sat still, his face white and taut. He knew now that it was all over. Tonight the ghetto walls would be broken down and mobs would run through the streets burning the synagogues, tearing down the houses and looting the rooms. He saw himself choosing which of his beautiful old books to take and

which to leave; he saw people hiding their children under piles of clothes in waggons so that if they got killed then at least their children might somehow escape. A great roar of confusion and terror, bloodshed and tears came up in his mind.

At that moment there was a noise outside the court. A jangling rumbling noise. The great doors at the end of the court were suddenly forced open. Everyone looked round. The judge stood up and Joseph the Golem drove a waggon straight into the courtroom. The horse reared up, people screamed. Joseph jumped down and walked

towards Rabbi Loeb. He was holding by the hand, Yana, the shabbes goya.

The court went into uproar. People were shouting and laughing. Levy ran over to Loeb and kissed him. Loeb was hugging Joseph. Yana was standing frightened and confused, looking at Dinah. Thaddeus was shrinking in his seat.

'Order! Order! Order!' shouted the judge. He had gathered who the young girl was. Quite clearly, there was no murder. No murder, no trial. He called for Loeb. The Rabbi explained everything as he understood it while Dinah and Thaddeus glanced about and shuffled their feet.

The judge turned to Dinah and Thaddeus and ordered the police to seize them. 'They shall be tried tomorrow,' he said and swept out of the court.

Rabbi Loeb cried. For once the whole thing had been too much for him. One moment he had been in such despair and the next he was happy beyond belief. He looked at big Joseph the Golem and it felt to him that he loved him as if he were his own son.

The next day at the trial, Dinah was put in prison for wrongfully accusing people of murder and lying in court while Thaddeus who had the protection of the church, was commanded to stay in his monastery till the day he died. Cut off from his people, unable to feed off the rumours and whispers, Thaddeus's powerful body seemed to crumple. His skin lost its brightness and for years he crept about the monastery like a damp shadow. No one knows when he finally died.

In the streets of the ghetto, people sang and danced.

CHAPTER FIFTEEN

The Warts

At long last the Jews were safe, Loeb thought. Little did he think that though the Jews were safe, Joseph the Golem could be in danger.

At this time, in Prague, if you wanted to insult someone and call him something horrible you called him a 'Nadler'. 'You Nadler,' people would say. It all came from some time earlier. A young man and woman got married and had children. One day it was discovered that the man, the woman and all the children all had a wart in exactly the same place on their bodies, just below the left breast. They hadn't realised when they got married they were born brother and sister, because they had lived apart, fostered by step parents. Shattered by the discovery, the family fell apart. Their name was Nadler and so the word 'Nadler' came to mean a wart. As a way of abusing someone, people would say to each other, 'You wart, you Nadler!'

When Loeb heard of this way of speaking he was furious. He would not have it that people insulted each other using someone else's misfortunes. In the central market place of the ghetto, a great horn was blown and, with two black candles burning, Rabbi Loeb announced that the word Nadler must never again be used as a nickname or an insult.

Most people accepted what he said and took care not to use the word again. Even so, there were still a few Jews in Prague who took no notice.

'He may be a good man, Rabbi Loeb,' they said, 'he may have done good things for us, but he can't tell us what we can and can't say in our own homes . . .'

One of these people was a man who carried boxes and crates for farmers who lived outside Prague. His name was David.

'If I want to call someone a Nadler, I'll call him a Nadler,' he said and he laughed with his farmer friends, who, to tell the truth thought the whole thing was a very strange Jewish business – a Rabbi telling people not to call each other 'Wart'. In fact, the word caught on with people like the farmers who weren't Jews.

Word reached Loeb that David was going around saying these things and so he sent Abraham the shammes off to call David to see him.

He was drinking with his farmer friends at the time and said, 'I will come when I am ready and not before.'

'Good on you, David, boy,' said the farmers. 'Stick up for yourself. Don't go just because some Nadler tells you to go.' And they all fell about laughing.

Rabbi Loeb was furious when he heard this and called Joseph the Golem. 'Joseph, fetch David the porter straightaway!'

Off went the Golem, found David still drinking with his friends, grabbed him from right out of the middle of them and, picking him up by the scruff of his neck, carried him back to Loeb. The punishment for disobeying a Rabbi in those days was a beating and that is what David the porter got.

'Now, David,' said the Rabbi,' promise here and now that you will never use the word Nadler again.'

David would have none of it. 'Nadler yourself. Nadler yourself,' he shouted. 'Don't you worry, Rabbi, I'll get my own back on the whole crowd of you. You think you rule everything now, don't you? You think you can behave like God Himself. Well you can't!'

Sore and humiliated, he went back to his farmer friends and told them the story. One of them had been at the court the day Dinah and Thaddeus had been shamed.

'This Joseph fellow is the danger,' said this farmer, 'if it wasn't for him, the good Father Thaddeus would be still preaching to us and showing us the way.'

David was too sore and angry to follow quite what the farmer was saying. All he knew was that he wanted revenge. The friends he was with were big and strong. They were just the kind who could take on Joseph the giant. David remembered the feeling of being dragged through the streets of Prague by that great silent man, when all he could do was flap his arms and legs about like some trapped ant.

'Right!' said David. 'We'll go for Joseph, the Rabbi's servant. Every Saturday night, at the end of Sabbath he goes to the well in Judah Meisel's garden. I'll meet you there.'

Sure enough, that Sabbath evening, the Golem came to Judah Meisel's garden. As Joseph lowered the bucket down deep into the well, out of the dark jumped four men – David and three farmers. Before Joseph could fight them off, they threw him head first down into the well.

It was a freezing cold night. Any human being would

have died in a matter of seconds but Joseph swam about; he tried to climb the walls. Up above, the men looked down and, though they could see nothing, they could hear him splashing about, so they hurled stones and bricks down the well. These struck Joseph, wounding his eyes and his shoulder. But he swam on, to and fro in the icy cold water. The men left him to die and went off into the night cuffing each other on the shoulders and laughing at such a good job done.

At Rabbi Loeb's house, people began to wonder what had become of Joseph. Finally, Loeb sent Abraham the shammes out to see what was going on. When he passed Judah Meisel's garden and heard the splashing, he shone his lantern down the well. Joseph saw the light and clapped his hands. Abraham lowered the well bucket, Joseph stepped into it, and Abraham heaved it up with Joseph on board. He was hurried home and put before a big warm fire.

With his hands, Joseph explained what had happened. Whatever Loeb didn't understand, he guessed. It seemed for a moment that Thaddeus was reaching them even from his imprisonment in the monastery. No matter though, Joseph had survived, a Golem is indestructible. But what should be done with these men?

Rabbi Loeb came up with a simple plan. Next day, Joseph went off in search of David the porter and the farmers. He found them sitting round their waggons at the end of the market. They were terrified to see him: what was this? Was he back from the dead? Would he drag them to his grave and bury them alive? They tried to escape but Joseph grabbed hold of them in his huge arms. He didn't threaten them, he didn't attack them. Instead, with a big smile on his face he hugged them, shook their hands, patted their necks, slapped their backs and pinched their cheeks as if they were long lost brothers. They pretended they were pleased to see him but inside they were both terrified and furious. After a good few minutes of this hugging and patting, Joseph waved them goodbye and strode off.

The men looked at each other; 'God help us, it was a ghost.'

'A demon more like.'

Between them they decided certainly the giant had risen from the dead and so it would be better not to have anything more to do with him. Hadn't they heard before that there was devil's business around the Rabbi and his servants?

A few days later strange things started to happen. Each of them began to come up in large black warts: on their necks, on their cheeks and on their hands. They didn't hurt, but they wouldn't go away either. They just squatted there for all to see. Suddenly none of the four men was quite so keen to call any one a Nadler. In fact, the word never passed their lips again and they went to their graves many years later still carrying the big black warts. They were quite sure that it was just as they feared – devil's work. What really happened was more simple. Rabbi Loeb had got Joseph to rub hands with poor old Leah, a good woman but warty. Warts are very catching, so when Joseph went down to the market place and gave David and the farmers a good hugging and pinching, he was really passing on warts by the bucket load. As you know, it stopped them calling people Nadler but it has to be said that secretly, there were people who did talk of David and his friends as 'The Last of the Nadlers'.

CHAPTER SIXTEEN

The Frenzy

A time of peace came for the Jews of Prague. They enjoyed this time when the Kaiser and the Cardinal wanted nothing more than to live side by side with the Jews in peace. Thaddeus was gone, the lies and rumours seemed to have died to a trickle and almost dried up altogether.

Every Friday night, the night before the Sabbath, Rabbi Loeb gave Joseph his tasks for the next day. No Jew was allowed to work on the Sabbath and giving Joseph orders would count as work and be against the Law too.

One Friday there didn't seem to be much for Joseph to do and so Loeb said to him, 'There is nothing for you to do tomorrow, you can do what you want.'

It was a slip of the tongue, because Joseph didn't have a mind that wanted or didn't want to do things and Loeb knew that more than anyone. It was just that, after all this time, he had almost come to think of Joseph as a real human being: a bit slow, not very clever but loving and kind. In the morning, Joseph was gone. No one was much bothered by this and went about their Sabbath affairs.

Outside, things were different. Joseph marched out on

to the street, picked up the first person he saw and hurled him through a window. He grabbed a sign off the wall and flung it to the ground. He kicked at a locked door which fell open and he walked in. It was a jeweller's workshop. With a great sweep of his arm, Joseph grabbed the jewels and flung them out of the window so hard they were lost from sight. As he walked out, he smashed the door frame to pieces. He picked up a plank and whacked it into the house over the road.

The house belonged to the baker.

Out he came. 'Joseph has gone mad!' he yelled.

But the Golem went on smashing at the bakery till he had broken the main beam and the whole house began to crack. He kicked and lunged at the house ripping the tiles off the roof. People came running but then stood about frightened and helpless. Joseph lurched towards the oven, still glowing from the evening before. He wrenched out the burning hot bricks, and flung them over his shoulder. On all sides, people screamed and wept. He scooped up hundreds of unsold cakes and loaves of bread and flung them out over the rooftops. Then with one mighty heave, he pulled the whole bakery down. The hot fire-bricks set light to the bread, the burning bread set light to the wood and soon the ruined bakery was on fire. Sparks flew up into the sky and leapt at the wooden frames next door. Still with his plank in his hand, Joseph swept out into the main market place, kicking and pushing as he went. His boots went straight through the door of the market peoples' store and apples, potatoes, turnips and carrots rolled about madly. Clothes went sailing through the air and people wailed. Was that a mad smile, someone noticed on Joseph's face? Anyone, anywhere near him was grabbed and flung like dolls in a playroom

as Joseph strode towards the ghetto gates. Oh no, what dangers would that lead to? If Joseph were to run out of the gates into the city of Prague and then run amok out there too, all the pent-up anger of the followers of Thaddeus would be heaped upon the Jews once again.

People screamed out at him, 'Joseph, stop, stop, stop!'

But he didn't hear. He saw the gates of the ghetto in front of him and seemed to set his mind on tearing them apart. Behind him, the fire roared and the wooden beams split and cracked. The hurt and wounded lay about moaning.

From the heart of the Altneuschul, the Old-New Synagogue, Rabbi Loeb heard the noise. At first he had preferred to stay praying, it was the Sabbath after all and why should he let others disturb him? But finally, he became angry: how dare they make such a noise? He rushed out ready to show his anger to whoever it was. But instead, a terrible sight lay before him. The ghetto was on fire, people lay about hurt and perhaps killed, others hid in doorways and Joseph himself was attacking the gates, heaving them off their hinges. Destruction and terror raged everywhere.

For a moment Loeb was trapped. It was the Sabbath, and wouldn't he be breaking Sabbath Law if he gave orders now? Loeb froze, watching the Golem heave the ghetto gates off the wall, lift them above his head and make ready to hurl them towards the city.

What jumped into Loeb's mind then, was the part of the Talmud where it is written, 'The law that Jews should keep the Sabbath must be put aside when human life is in danger. Break the Sabbath to save someone's life.' Wasn't this a time like that?

'Joseph, stop where you are,' shouted the Rabbi.

At once Joseph stopped. He very gently laid down the ghetto gates as if they were children he loved.

'Come here,' said Loeb.

Joseph walked towards the Rabbi, without so much as a look at the wreckage and pain around him.

'Go home to bed,' said the Rabbi.

Turning to his friends, he said, 'Joseph could have destroyed all of Prague, if I hadn't stopped him.'

For the first time, the people of the ghetto were angry with their Rabbi. Many were furious. They crowded round him, their eyes still showing the terror they felt when Joseph rampaged amongst them. In the market square, people were limping away home, others still lay broken and bleeding on the hard paving stones.

'Now, what?' shouted Shimon the baker, shaking with fear and anger. 'What are you going to do about this maniac? This beast?'

'Give me time, give me time,' said Loeb.

'Time? You want time?' yelled Shimon. 'Years of work have just been burnt up in one moment here. Don't talk to me about time,' and he fell to the ground crying helplessly.

'Get rid of that Joseph,' said someone. 'Get rid of him or we are cursed forever.'

'Give me time,' said Loeb again.

' "Chaliera zol im chappen" – may he be struck down with the plague,' said one.

'Head in a coffin, coffin in the earth,' said another.

'Enough,' said the Rabbi. 'Believe me, I will do what is right for all of us.' And he turned and made his way back to the Altneuschul.

'Now we don't need to be afraid of one of *their* maniacs,' said Misha the fool pointing to the Prague beyond the ghetto gates, 'we've got one all of our own.'

'Now the clearing up begins, more like,' said his friend.

'Such a mess only a Golem could clear up,' said Misha the fool.

Someone laughed.

CHAPTER SEVENTEEN

The End

The next day, Rabbi Loeb was deeply troubled. A change had come over his life. He wandered round the house feeling strange until he came to Joseph still lying in bed, where he had been sent. He looked at him stretched out there and new feelings came over him. Before the disaster, Loeb felt grateful and loving towards Joseph. As long as Joseph had done what he had been asked he was part of the family. But now he had gone beserk, Loeb was reminded that Joseph was nothing more than what he had said at the very beginning: like a pump or a mill working away to orders from him. He was just a body that did whatever Loeb asked him to do. Though underneath, was there perhaps a strange part of the Golem that wanted to break and destroy? Some part of him that not even Loeb could really control? Of course, yesterday, he had stopped when he was asked, but what if one day he didn't? What if he was developing some kind of mind of his own? What would that mind be like?

At that moment, Joseph woke and stood up, his head way above the Rabbi's. For the first time, Loeb was afraid. Up until then he had always felt safe and secure with Joseph around, as if he was a massive bodyguard. But now he felt as if Joseph was a great towering danger. The people in the market-place were right: he had to be got rid of.

Once again, Loeb turned to his books. How was it to be done? As he pored over the papers, he noticed that the door to his study was slightly open. Through the gap he could see Joseph sitting by the table in the passage. His face neither happy nor sad, just blank. Looking out of the window watching people as they passed the house.

How strange it is, thought Loeb, that I'm in here reading how to destroy you and you neither know nor could understand anything about it.

After much reading and thinking, Rabbi Loeb called on Abraham the shammes and his pupil Jacob Sasson. When they were all together, he called for Joseph. Just as it had been when he was created, it was midnight.

'Joseph,' said the Rabbi, 'Go to the Altneuschul, the Old-New Synagogue, and climb up into the attic and wait for us there.'

Joseph got up and left the house. There was one small part of Rabbi Loeb that wondered – would Joseph do exactly as he was told? Did the Golem have a mind of its own now?

The three men watched Joseph cross the square, then they left the house and followed him, bringing candles. The great synagogue was quiet and hollow, carrying every whisper and shuffle round and round its walls. Joseph was nowhere to be seen.

'He must have gone up to the attic already,' said Loeb. 'Come.'

Leading the way, Loeb held the candles high, and the three men climbed up the steps into the attic. When they got there Joseph was waiting for them, standing in the dark, his hands on his hips.

'We have to change what it says on his forehead,' said Loeb. 'We have to take the "E" off "EMET" to make it say "MET". Then it will no longer mean "TRUTH" but will mean "DEAD".'

They stood looking at Joseph and wondering how they were going to manage it. He was so much taller than they were. They couldn't reach his nose, let alone his forehead.

'Bend down, Joseph,' said the Rabbi.

The Golem didn't move. Loeb felt his heart quicken.

'Joseph, bend down!'

The Golem just stood there, towering over them in the dark attic. Why wouldn't he move? It was as if he suspected what was going to happen. Loeb was aware of Abraham the shammes and Jacob Sasson taking a little step backwards. They were remembering Joseph running amok in the square. He looked at them with his big blank face.

'Joseph,' said the Rabbi, 'take off my shoes.'

Joseph bent down. His head came right up to Loeb's chest. Loeb raised his hand to rub out the 'E' but stopped. He looked straight into Joseph the Golem's eyes and for a brief moment felt again what he had felt that day the Golem had ridden straight into the court with Yana, the shabbes goya. Should a father destroy his own son? he was asking himself.

Joseph had taken off one of the Rabbi's shoes and was about to start on the other.

'Joseph,' said the Rabbi, 'you saved us.'

The blank face looked up at the Rabbi for a moment more and in that moment Loeb raised his finger to Joseph's forehead and rubbed out the 'E'. Silently and

slowly, the Golem sank to the floor, rolled back and lay motionless looking up at the rafters of the old attic.

'Joseph? Joseph?' whispered the Rabbi scarcely believing that this was the end. 'Can you hear me?'

There was silence.

Then, with a slight break in his voice, Loeb said, 'We do everything we did when we created him but the other way round.'

They stood at the Golem's head instead of his feet. They said the words backwards, they walked round the Golem backwards and in the opposite direction.

When they had finished, they knelt down to look at Joseph. He was nothing but a hard mud statue. Then Loeb gathered up some old prayer books, shawls and Rabbi's robes that were stored in the attic of the Altneuschul and the three of them covered the mud figure. They went home to their beds, thinking of the last few years and the strange and miraculous things the Golem had done.

In the morning, Rabbi Loeb announced that Joseph had gone.

'He has disappeared from town and is nowhere to be found.'

Only the three men and the people they confided in, their wives and children, knew the whole truth. For hundreds of years, father to son, mother to daughter, they passed on the secret, so for generations only a few people knew that the Golem lay under the old shawls and prayer books in the attic of the Altneuschul.

CHAPTER EIGHTEEN

The Grave

Not many years ago, another story of where the Golem lies, came to light. Abraham the shammes had listened carefully to all that Rabbi Loeb said and did down by the river the night the Golem was created. He knew where the Golem was now. Over the months and years, an urge nagged away inside Abraham – couldn't he, a little old shammes that no one ever took much notice of, awaken the Golem? And isn't Ascher, that clever son-in-law of mine, studying and studying away at the Kabbala? With all this, Abraham thought, how can I fail? I'll have a Golem all of my very own. Then they'll know I'm really something. With a Golem as my servant, the world will be mine.

One night he began to make preparations. Off he went to the Altneuschul. He got as far as the bottom of the steps but was overcome with fear at what destruction he would let loose if something went wrong. What if the Golem wouldn't take orders and started off again, rampaging all over the city?

He ran home, having frightened himself off doing anything. But the nagging urge to meddle with magic bothered away at him some more. A few days later he told his brother in law, what he was thinking. He was called Abraham too and he was the shammes at the Pinkas synagogue. Difficult! There were two of them called Abraham the shammes. What to do about it? This Abraham they called Pinkas.

Anyway, never mind what he was called, he was interested in this affair and the night after Pinkas heard what was on Abraham's mind, both men climbed the steps into the attic of the Altneuschul. In the dark they heaved off all the old shawls and prayer books and there staring at them from the floor was the huge clay figure of the Golem. They lifted it from its resting place, staggered downstairs with it and took it across to the Pinkas synagogue. What a sight! Two men running through the streets at night carrying a lifeless giant. They terrified themselves with the thought that, at any moment, it could come alive by itself. Or perhaps by moving it, they would meet up with a 'dybbuk', a spirit, and the dybbuk would, God forbid, enter the Golem's body.

But nothing happened, the Golem stayed a statue. So, in the Pinkas synagogue, they hid it behind the 'Alemor', the reading desk, and then scampered home thankful that so far, so good.

The next day, Abraham called on his son-in-law, Ascher, and told him what was going on.

'I need your help, Ascher, with all your Kabbala knowledge. The business of which way round the Golem we walked, I remember; the business with the message on his forehead, that too I remember. But the chants, the charms, they're another story.'

Ascher set to reading the 'Book of Creation' to find out what had to be said and sung. After several days, young

Ascher was sure he had them by heart. So now, the three men, Abraham the shammes, Pinkas and Ascher were ready to awaken Joseph the Golem.

At the Pinkas synagogue, they heaved the clay figure out and dragged it through the streets and alleys in the dead of night to Ascher's house. Then they carried it down into his cellar and began the ceremony. Round and round they walked, chanting. They stopped, they waited.

It seemed for one quick second that Joseph began to stir but it was only the shadow of the candle changing. No – Joseph the Golem stayed just where he was. Night after night the three men tried to arouse him. They tried all the chants and charms they could. They walked this way, that way round the figure; they tried chanting loud, they tried chanting soft. They sang the charms, they shouted them, but the figure never stirred. Not one flicker – not one shudder. Abraham the shammes was shattered.

At this time a terrible plague raged through Prague. Thousands of people were struck down. The sound of people gripped with fever screeched out of the houses and filled the streets. Two of Ascher's children died. Ascher's wife knew why: the Golem in the cellar put a curse on the poor things.

'Ascher take it away, take it away before it puts the curse on more of us. God forbid that it should happen. Haven't we suffered enough?'

The bodies of the two children were washed and prepared for their coffins but Ascher secretly, put both of them in one coffin. Then he took an axe and hacked off the arms, legs and head of the Golem and crammed the broken pieces into the other coffin. He hired a waggon from David the porter and, that night, took the coffins out of the city to the graveyard for people who had died of the plague. What a place! Freshly dug graves everywhere, many unmarked with any stone or memorial; open pits with bodies rotting in heaps; the trickle of water seeping in on them all.

In such a place, Abraham and Pinkas buried the two children squashed into the one coffin. With hardly a word between them, they rode their waggon up to Gallows' hill, for years the place where the criminals and murderers of Prague had been buried. If the Golem was a body that could house a dybbuk or a demon, now was the time it would happen. Abraham and Pinkas muttered their prayers as the waggon rolled up the hill.

One mile, two hundred yards from Prague's Neustatter Gate, on the Vienna State Road, on the city side, Abraham and Pinkas buried the Golem. Not a sound came from inside the coffin: not a scratch, not a creak. They hurled earth on to it so hard and so fast, it was as if they were burying a dangerous criminal.

The night was the night of the 5th Adar of the Jewish calendar, and there, say the old papers, lie the remains of Joseph the Golem.

CHAPTER NINETEEN

The Death

Every night at midnight Rabbi Loeb recited a prayer and then crossed to the Altneuschul with Abraham to talk with the spirits of the dead. Abraham waited in the little room at the side of the synagogue. After an hour of talking, Rabbi Loeb went home and slept till the morning. On the night of the 11th Elul 5369, in the Jewish calender, Rabbi Loeb did as he had always done, but the moment he fell asleep he had a terrifying dream.

He saw himself standing in a great courtyard. The gate was open. At one end, in front of a kind of altar, stood a huge figure dressed in a grey cloak. His face was the same colour as his cloak, but bony and shiny. From his eyes seemed to come flashes of lightning. In his hand, he held a knife and from it dripped blood. A long line of young men stood near him waiting to be slaughtered by this appalling figure. Then Loeb realised he knew the young men: they were his own pupils from his class at the synagogue. They all looked towards him sadly, appealing to him. He felt overcome with pity and sadness himself. The terrible giant began stabbing and killing each man in turn. There was blood everywhere. Suddenly he caught sight of his son-in-law, Isaac ben Simson, and then his favourite, Jacob ben Sasson, the men who had helped him make the Golem. He saw the creature reach out for Isaac. Loeb dashed forward and snatched the knife from his hand.

'Stop, you destroyer. Stop these murders!'

And he woke up.

Terrified, Loeb sat up and looked around him, the dream was still in his head: The terrible grey giant, the long line of his pupils, the frightful murders, the bleeding knife. He began to tremble, leapt out of bed and next moment found himself washing his hands. Washing and washing. Now he began striding up and down the room. Wasn't this another warning? After all these years of peace and happiness, did it mean that now, in his old age, they were threatened all over again? His mind went back to Joseph the Golem. Perhaps he shouldn't have taken the life out of him after all. Perhaps he would need to raise him up to live again. Loeb saw in his mind's eye, the mud figure of Joseph lying, as he thought, in the attic of the Altneuschul.

Suddenly, his eye caught sight of the Altneuschul over the road. It was lit up. What is going on there at this unearthly hour, he thought. It must be another plot against us. Someone is busy with blood or a dead body. Oh no. Not again.

Loeb woke up Abraham, 'Quick, take the keys,' he said. 'Follow me.'

As fast as they could, they rushed to the synagogue.

The Rabbi unlocked the doors, and while Abraham stepped into the little room at the side, Loeb strode into the main part of the synagogue. The sight that met his eyes made the hairs on the back of his neck prickle. The very same grey giant he had seen in his dream was stand-

ing at the reading table. In his right hand was the same bloody knife and in his left hand was a long scroll. On it were names, written in blood. The terrible figure moved his lips and called out the names one after another. Rabbi Loeb listened.

They were the names of the people Loeb had seen in his dream, the same people this unknown giant had slaughtered in his dream. Now the Rabbi knew who the giant figure was. This was the Angel of Death. Rabbi Loeb sprang forward and snatched the scroll out of his hand. The Angel of Death stood motionless – calm and still.

Loeb turned and began to run for the doors, praying that the Angel wouldn't chase him. In the little room, Abraham was trembling all over. He had heard the terrible one call out *his* name. But now Loeb had the scroll in his hand and, like a warrior returning from a battle he has won, he carried the scroll back to his house with it tucked in his robe.

There, he read the names. Over and over again, he read them to see who he had saved. Yes, he had saved them all. He went through in his mind's eye, all the people in his dream, and yes, they were all here. He felt a great surge of pride in his chest – he had saved all his friends and pupils. He just couldn't stop himself reading that scroll, over and over again. Yes, yes, yes, he had saved them all from the Angel of Death.

Suddenly, in the middle of one of these readings, he noticed that one part of the scroll was damaged. He glanced down. A part of it had been torn off. It was the corner of the scroll that the Angel of Death was holding in his hand when Loeb snatched it. Then he noticed little markings around the tear. Loeb realised what this meant:

on the torn-off corner that the Angel of Death still held in his hand was one more name. But whose name could it be? Loeb thought and thought but really couldn't guess. Again he went over and over the names on the list, trying to think who could this person be? The scroll contained all the members of his class; there wasn't a single person missing. Who could it be? He even found himself thinking of the Golem. Could the Angel of Death have got it wrong and thought that it was *his* job to destroy the Golem? The Rabbi was amused thinking of it.

A week passed. All his pupils at the synagogue were well. Loeb was quite sure now that he had saved them from death. On the seventh day, he held a feast to celebrate what had happened. At the feast, he told them of all the strange events that had occurred in the last few days. They were delighted and talked and sang till late.

Soon after, Rabbi Loeb caught a cold. The cold got worse and worse, spread to his chest; a fever gripped his body, until, on the 18th of Elul 5369, Rabbi Judah Loeb died. On the torn-off corner of paper that the Angel of Death had held on to had been the name, Judah Loeb! In looking at that scroll over and over again, trying to think of the missing name, Loeb forgot his own. He whose name was last on the sheet was the first to go.

And so ended an extraordinary time in the history of Prague.